"Never let the truth get in the wa... good story." M...

I hope you...

Backyard Bigfoot

(The Norfolk files Book One)

by Mark Woods

Copyright: Mark Woods. 2020.
Black Hart publications.

ALL RIGHTS RESERVED. This book contains material protected under International copyright law and any unauthorised reprint or use of this material in any way, shape or form is prohibited. No part of this book, including the cover and photos, may be reproduced or transmitted in any form or by any means, electronic or mechanical, including photocopying, recording, or any information storage and retrieval system without express written permission from the author/publisher.

Any resemblance to any persons, living, dead, or undead, or any places or locations in real life is purely coincidental.

No Bigfoot were hurt in the production of this book.

The same cannot be said for any humans.

This book is dedicated, as always, to Catt Dahman for first starting me off on this crazy ride, but also to the real life Amy Hayden, whom I first met playing Friday the 13th online – you wanted me to write you in as a character in one of my books, so I did. I only hope you enjoy what I've done to you as payback for you killing me as Jason all those times!

This book originally started off life as a short story, but somewhere along the lines I realised it had so much more potential to be extended into a full length novella. Eagle eyed readers may note I have taken a few geographical liberties with the real-life Thetford Forest, but I make no apologies for that.

As for the Thetford Bigfoot? There have been numerous sightings over the last twenty years, a couple of which provided inspiration for this story.

Does this mean there's really something out there?

I don't know.

But I know I won't be wandering around out there all alone after dark, that's all I'm saying…

Sparkymarky, June 2020

Prelude

<u>June 1986.</u>

Darren Matthews, his wife, Emma, and their eleven year old son, Russell, were all driving back from a visit to the mother-in-law's, travelling down the A1075 late at night, when they encountered what would later become known as The Wild-man of Watton.
His mum and dad were arguing *again*, whilst Russell sat in the backseat with his headphones on, but he could still hear them bickering even over the music he was listening to. His mum was busy moaning something about how his dad had never liked her mother, whilst his dad was trying tactfully to deny it without actually lying, when something ran across the road straight in front of them. The car clipped whatever it was, hard, as the they went past, with a loud and almighty bang that caused Russell to look up from his music as he felt the car shake with the sudden impact.
"Oh God…oh God…oh God…was that…was that a bear?" Emma asked, and then realising the foolishness of what she had just said – for this was the U.K and over here there *were* no bears – "or…or a person? Oh God, Darren…did you just…hit somebody? What have I told you about keeping your eyes on the road and always concentrating while you are driving?"
Well, if you hadn't been having such a go at me…was what Darren started to say, but then stopped himself just in time.
This was neither the time, nor the place.
Not right now.
"It was probably just a deer," he said instead. "A really large Muntjac or something…" though even as he said this, Darren had his doubts. He'd only had the briefest glimpse of what he'd hit back there in the darkness, but by the light of his headlights, he'd thought for a second that he'd seen a tall, hominid figure covered in fur, with a long snout, just before they'd – *he'd* - struck it in passing.
"We have to go back," Emma insisted, but, "You have to be joking," Darren responded. They had stayed at her mum's for much longer than he'd intended, and then left late to boot, which is why it was now so dark out and all Darren really wanted right about now was to get home because, quite frankly, he had well and truly had enough.
But his wife *did* kind of have a point, he eventually conceded. If he *had* struck a living animal and left it lying by the side of the road, injured, it was only fair he turn around and go back, he supposed, if only to put the poor creature out of its suffering and help end its misery.

Besides, though his rational mind was doing its damnedest to reject and refute what he'd thought he'd seen, still another part of him was not entirely convinced that he *hadn't* hit a person back there and if that *were* the case, then he really needed to go back and check - if only so he could notify the authorities and possibly even the emergency services in the case that whoever he'd hit might be in need of urgent medical assistance.

"Okay, okay, fine, we'll head back," Darren said, reluctantly, and found somewhere safe so they could turn around.

"Dad, what are we doing?" Russell asked from the back-seat, finally looking up from his Sony cassette player and noticing that something was amiss.

He had barely registered the impact before going back to his music but a smart kid, now he was starting to sense something was wrong.

"It's nothing, sweetheart – just taking a little detour," his mother told him, looking back and smiling at him sweetly, and that was when Russell knew something really *was* wrong, because his mother never normally called him 'sweetheart.'

Never.

As they drove back, slowly, past the point in the road where Darren was sure he'd hit the creature, both Emma and Darren stared out the side window, looking for any sign of whatever it was he'd struck. Thankfully, at this time of night, there wasn't all that much traffic behind them and it wasn't long before they passed the place where whatever it was they had hit had run out into the road.

There was a lay-by on the opposite side, and so Darren took this opportunity to turn around again and pull in so that they were facing back the way they had originally been headed.

He switched off the engine.

"What are you doing?" Emma asked, and then from the back Russell's voice also chipped in, "Yeah, dad, what's going on?"

"I'm just going to go have a little look-see, see if I can spot whatever it was I hit. That's what you wanted isn't it?"

Darren undid his seatbelt, reached over and pulled out a torch from the glovebox nearest his wife, and made to open the door.

"Wait here…and lock the doors," he told them both, turning back to face them.

"Seriously?" Emma asked him. "You're just going to gallivant off into the night and leave the both of us sitting here, waiting for you? I don't think so."

She made to undo her own seatbelt. "I'm coming with you."

"Me too," came a voice from the back, as Darren and Emma both turned around to face him and simultaneously said, "no."

"Awwww…dad…." Russell whined, but both his parents stood firm.

"No way," Emma told him. "We have no idea what's out there, and if it *is* a wounded animal, then it might not be safe."

"Your mum's right for once, kiddo," Darren said. "You're better off staying here. Just keep the doors locked while we're gone, okay? We won't be five minutes…"

The pair of them left the car, locking it behind them, exited the lay-by and started heading down the side of the road towards where Darren thought he had struck whatever it was that had ran out in the road – guided only by the light of the torch he had taken from the car.

They had gone no more than a few yards before they both realised that, despite their instructions, Russell had also left the car and was following them.

"I thought we told you to wait in the car," Darren hissed at him.

"I want to see too," Russell replied in response. This was the most exciting thing to have happened to him all day and no way was he about to miss this. Russell hated going to his Nan's, thought he was too old now to accompany his parents on their visits, and would spend most of his time when he was there with his head stuck in a book.

He was looking forward to hitting twelve in a few months, because with any luck his parents might finally come around to the idea that he was old enough to stay home alone on his own and hopefully, might even actually consider leaving him behind when they went to see his Nan.

In the meantime though, he thought, no way was he about to be left behind in the car like an unruly child when there was a chance to accompany his parents on the closest thing to an adventure he was ever likely to get.

Darren looked at Emma in the darkness in an attempt to ask her non-verbally what her advice was, but his wife just shrugged at him in the torchlight as if to say, '*it's your decision. It's entirely up to you.*'

"Fine, you're here now, let's just go," Darren finally conceded. "But stay close, and no wandering off – this is a busy road."

Russell looked back at him as if to say, '*really? Busy? Like seriously?*' because the roads were still empty and there was not a single car in sight, but he did as he was told anyway because he didn't want to push his luck and get himself escorted back to the car.

Darren stopped by a break in the bushes.

By the torchlight, he thought he could make out blood on the branches, like something wounded or hurt had pushed its way through in an attempt to escape whatever had struck it.

"Here," he said. "Whatever it was we smacked, I think it went through here…"

He pushed his way through the brush, trying to follow the crude trail the animal or whatever had made. Just beyond the bushes was a steep drop down into a ditch and beyond that, the start of Thetford Forest.

"Wait here," Darren said. "I'm just going to head down there and take a look in case whatever it was is down there, hurt. You guys stay up here, take the torch, and shine it down there so I can see where I'm going…"

He started down the steep slope.

About half-way down, his foot got caught in a small hole in the dark, and Darren lost his balance. He ended up half-sliding/ half-tumbling the rest of the way down into the ditch, landing in something soft at the bottom.

Something soft…and something squishy.

Something that smelled…dead.

The remains of a dead deer, he suddenly realised, and one that from the look and feel of it was half-eaten. Maybe whatever he had hit *had* been a bear, he suddenly thought, and it had been crossing the road with its dinner.

Though he had dismissed Emma's comment out of hand earlier, as had she the minute she said it, now that he thought of it, Darren thought he recalled reading something about the unconfirmed sighting of a bear out here in Thetford Forest a few years ago now. He remembered it, because he recalled thinking at the time that it made a change from all the big cat sightings you normally heard about in these parts – reports that Darren thought were every bit as unlikely as a bear living out here in the middle of sleepy old Norfolk..

Something that now suddenly seemed a whole lot more believable in the dark.

"What is it?" Emma called down from somewhere up above him, back up near the road. "Did you find something?" and then almost as an after-thought, "Are you okay? Did you hurt yourself down there when you fell? Please don't tell me I need to go back to the lay-by and call you an ambulance."

"I'm fine," Darren called back. "I might be a little bruised, but it's more my pride that's hurt than anything else. I did find *something* down here though – a dead deer. Must have been what I struck, like I told you."

Darren elected not to tell her that he didn't think that *was* what he'd hit, nor that from what little he could see and feel in the dark, the deer appeared to have been something else's dinner.

As far as he was concerned, he just wanted to put this whole darn incident behind him, get back on the road, and travel the last few dozen miles or so back home. He really had had about enough for one day now, even more *now* than earlier on, and the last thing he wanted was to carry on searching down here in the dark in what was essentially a wild goose chase.

Darren pushed himself up to his feet and prepared himself to face climbing the slope again but before he did, he paused to take one last look behind him as, for

one second, he thought he heard something big, and heavy, moving through the undergrowth very close by him.
A pair of bright red eyes suddenly lit up in the darkness in front of him.
A smell of carrion, and dead flesh – much more powerful than that he had smelled on the dead deer a few moments ago - hit his nostrils as whatever it was that was stood in front of him, approximately seven feet tall by his guess, opened its mouth and slowly breathed out what sounded like the beginning of a growl.
Darren felt his bladder starting to let go.
He was not entirely sure what it was that stood in front of him, but in that moment he was sure it was no bear.
He did not know why he thought that exactly, but he did.
He did not know what it was stood in front of him.
All he knew was that it was time to go.
Darren sprinted back up the slope, much more gracefully than his descent, and thankfully somehow managing to avoid the hole he had tripped over before that had sent him tumbling, and reached the top where his wife and son were still waiting for him.
"Go," he breathed, gasping for breath, close to hyperventilating with fear at the thought of whatever it was behind him that, for all he knew, could even now be climbing back up the slope after them all.
"Go," he urged his wife and son again, "get back to the car, quickly, and don't look back."
"What is it?" Emma asked, seeing the abject expression of fear upon his face by the powerful torch that she held. She didn't think she ever remembered seeing him so scared in all the time that they had both been married.
"Just do what I say, both of you," Darren snapped, and his tone of voice spurred them both into doing what he'd told them, with no more questions asked.
The three of them hurried to the car, and then Darren locked them all inside. Starting the engine, he turned in his seat to look back at Russell in the back.
"Everyone strapped in?" He asked, and Russell and Emma both nodded.
Darren pulled the car back out of the lay-by and swung them out into the road.
"What was it back there? What did you see?" Emma asked him again as he drove, still insistent on some kind of answer.
"Doesn't matter what I saw…or what I thought I saw…" Darren told her. "I don't want to talk about it, alright? Let's just get home and forget all this ever happened."
The three of them drove off into the night.

They never noticed the single pair of eyes that stood there, watching them from the side of the road as they drove past. Or if they did, not a one of them said a word…

***

This was rapidly turning into one hell of a year, P.C Chris Jennings thought next morning, as he stood where the young family last night claimed to have seen what could only have been some kind of bear, and scratched his head.
And what was worse, it was only June.
So far this year, this part of the U.K had seen massive electrical storms that had caused all sorts of power outages throughout all of Norfolk and Suffolk; experienced massive, huge great chunks of hail the size of which were unprecedented and the like of which had never been seen before, and now this.
Bears.
In Norfolk.
Who would've have thought it.
The father of the family, who had been driving, had claimed he'd hit the beast and struck it with his car, and then gone for a look to see what he'd hit, and had insisted what he's seen *hadn't* been a bear.
But the brief description he had given of the creature he'd thought he'd seen matched that of a bear and if that *hadn't* been what he'd hit, then what else could it possibly have been?
P.C Jennings had heard the rumours of some kind of Bigfoot that was supposed to live out here in Thetford Forest - of course he had, everyone had - but he'd always dismissed them out of hand because everyone knew there was no such thing as Bigfoot, right?
Especially not in sleepy old Norfolk.
No, much more likely it was definitely a bear of some sort – maybe a pet that had escaped, or some kind of refugee from a circus or something that had been left behind by mistake, and had then migrated out into the wild to live out its days deep in the heart of Thetford Forest.
Chris Jennings knew this area, and knew it well, and so it hadn't taken him long to pinpoint the lay-by where the father had insisted he'd parked last night. The lay-by lay close to the end of the main Watton to Thetford road, better known as the A1075, not far from where the main part of Thetford Forest began.
From there, it was only a short walk to the spot where the man had allegedly fallen down into a ditch, and then supposedly encountered the 'bear.'
Now, as Chris drew level with the steep slope the man claimed to have fallen down last night, he slowly and carefully began to make his descent.

Upon reaching the bottom, Chris looked around but could see no sign of the dead deer the father claimed to have stumbled upon in the darkness. Instead, stretching off out into the forest, was a thick, heavy trail where it looked very much like something – possibly the deer - had been dragged off into the undergrowth.
Dried blood on the leaves of the trees seemed to back up this assumption – indicating P.C Jennings was almost certainly in the right spot.
Hesitating for a moment to contemplate whether he should call for back-up, and then deciding against it, Jennings began following the trail.
As one of the youngest officers at the station, P.C Chris Jennings had kind of drawn the short straw when the report about the alleged 'bear' had come in. No-one really believed the father had seen anything - many thinking he had just been spooked by a passing stag or a deer, the rest, no doubt, the result of an entirely over-active imagination – but standard procedure dictated his case be taken seriously and at the very least, investigated, and so Jennings had been nominated to head out here and take a look, even though it would probably just end up turning out to be a complete waste of police resources.
If Jennings radioed for back-up, and then ended up producing nothing to show for it, he would become a laughing stock amongst his fellow colleagues and probably never live it down. No, better to continue to investigate on his own, he decided, for if nothing else, it beat being back at the station filling out paperwork or doing traffic reports.
Thick fog was starting to descend from out of the trees, covering the whole area in white. The fog appeared to have emerged from out of nowhere, for it had been perfectly clear when he had arrived, and the whole thing gave the forest a spooky atmosphere where it was easy to imagine anything were possible. *Even Bigfoot…*
Stop it, Jennings told himself. *Everyone knows Bigfoot isn't real, is just an urban myth – just like the Loch Ness Monster, or that creature that was supposed to live out on Pentney Lakes…*
The trail opened up into a clearing in the trees.
A series of burnt, ragged tree trunks lined the clearing – scorched where they had obviously at some point been struck by lightning.
On one of these trunks, the bloody head of a disembodied stag had crudely been impaled. Below it, exhibited almost in some kind of cruel and callous display, was what was obviously the rest of the creature's disembowelled body – opened up so that its insides, its guts and intestines, all lay spilled out all around it. Flies buzzed as they fed on the corpse, and the stench of death and decay filled the air.

At the sight of the gruesome vision before him, P.C Jennings turned and retched into the grass behind him – instantly feeling sickened and disgusted at what he'd just stumbled across out here in the woods.

Still feeling nauseous, reluctantly Jennings forced himself to turn back to the corpse and the disembodied head for a second look, in a bid to try and discover any evidence as to what might possibly have been responsible.

*Bigfoot…it's Bigfoot, I tell you…*his inner voice spoke up inside his head, but Jennings wisely chose to ignore it.

The dead stag almost looked like it was staring at him, he thought. Though its eyes were glassy, and clouded, and devoid and empty of any and all signs of life, he still couldn't shake the feeling the stag was looking at him, even though he knew that was physically impossible.

Slowly, he started to back away from the clearing – uncertain exactly what he had just stumbled across, but not wanting to stay here any longer than was absolutely necessary - but the sound of something huge, suddenly moving amongst the trees, somewhere close behind him, momentarily caused him to stop.

There was something out there, he thought, moving just behind the tree-line; several somethings in fact, hidden by both the trees and the thick, heavy fog all around him.

I should probably get out of here, Jennings thought, but he had the distinct feeling he was slowly being surrounded.

More movement came from just beyond the trees.

Something out there howled, and the noise sent shivers down P.C Jennings's spine. The sound was like nothing he had ever heard before.

More answering howls and cries came from the woods all around him and now, Jennings was even more certain than ever he was slowly being circled by whatever it was that was out there.

If he didn't get out of here and right now, he thought, *chances were he'd end up just like the stag.*

As quick as he was able, P.C Jennings turned and fled from the forest, back the way he'd come - the sound of pursuit following him all the way back to the road.

Once back at his car, Jennings finally radioed for back-up.

***

When reinforcements eventually arrived, Jennings led them back to the clearing he had found but by the time they got there, the disembowelled body and the head of the stag were both gone.

Blood, and discarded pieces of entrails, littered the clearing and the whole site closely resembled the kind of scene you might expect to see in an abattoir, but of the corpse itself there was no sign.

"It was here, I'm telling you," Jennings insisted to his Superintendent, who had also come out here with some of Jennings's fellow officers.

"Well, there's nothing here now," his Superintendent curtly told him, obviously annoyed at having his precious time wasted on what now appeared to be nothing but a wild goose chase.

Well, a wild bear chase anyway…

Jennings saw one of his fellow officers raising his hand in a drinking motion behind his Superintendent, indicating Jennings as he did so, causing another of his colleagues to laugh out loud at his expense.

"Thank-you for wasting my time, P.C Jennings," his Superintendent told him. "I'll see *you* back at the station."

He stormed off back to his car, parked with the others back at the lay-by. Jennings's colleagues went after him, shaking their heads as they did so. Jennings stayed for a minute to look back at the tree-line.

Something had been out there earlier, he was sure of it, he thought, but he had the strong sense that whatever it had been was long gone now.

Already anticipating the ridicule he would face back at the station, Jennings reluctantly turned and followed the others back to his car.

It would be several years before anyone sighted the mysterious Bigfoot of Thetford Forest again…

One

December 2007

It was over two decades later.

Frank and Amy were out camping in Thetford Forest when they had their own encounter with the creature that, over the years, had become known locally as The Wild-man of Watton, The Bigfoot of Thetford Forest, or sometimes just as The Beast of the A1075.

Amy had experienced a miscarriage over a year ago, and had still not fully gotten over her loss. Frank had just been made redundant from his job when the banking firm he worked for had shut down their local branch and with Amy still not yet working, a couple of days camping, canoeing and fishing was the only holiday they could afford.

Their first day was entirely uneventful.

Frank and Amy had found somewhere safe and secure to leave their car, a now ageing but still reliable, trusty 4x4, and then hiked out into the forest to camp out under the trees and the stars.

Frank thought a few days of peace and tranquillity would do Amy good. Since the miscarriage, his wife was a changed woman – a shadow of her former self, and no longer the woman he had married. It had been a little over eighteen months since she had lost their baby – *their* baby, not just hers – and he couldn't help thinking she should probably have long started the slow road to recovery and getting back to some form of normality by now.

But by the same extent, he was not a complete arsehole.

He also appreciated that whatever sense of loss he thought he had experienced, it must be a lot harder for her – after all, it had been *her* body that had been carrying their child and in the end, it had been *her* body that had ultimately rejected it.

That was the kind of thing, he thought, that he supposed one didn't just '*get over*' – but at the same time, Frank wanted his old wife back.

The woman he had fallen in love with all those years ago when they first met. The only woman who had ever been able to make him laugh, and genuinely laugh out loud, and the one woman who could always make him smile – even, and especially, when he was in the foulest of moods.

This last year or so, Frank felt almost as though he had been living with a ghost – a ghost of their former marriage – and this, this little trip, was his way of attempting to try and bring back a little bit of the woman he loved.

Already, on the journey out here, he had already seen a change in her.

The closer they had got to the forest, the more she had seemed to come out of herself – even starting to show a little excitement at the thought of roughing it for a few days and getting back to nature.

But then, she had always enjoyed camping – which was why he had decided to bring her out here in the first place.

They could have used some of his redundancy package to afford a 'proper' holiday if they'd really chosen to, he supposed, but then they had no idea just yet what the future had in store for them, nor how long it might take him to find another job.

For Amy was adamant she was not ready yet to go back to a job teaching primary school children again, and the last thing Frank wanted to do was try and force her into going back to work because, he knew, if he did, that really would be the death knell of their marriage and right now, that same union was hanging by a tenuous enough thread as it was.

Frank and Amy found somewhere nice to set up camp for the night, and then made love for the first time in eighteen months under the stars.
It had all been as close to perfect, Frank thought later, as it ever could have been.
It was the next day when everything all started to go downhill...

**

The second day started off just as well.
Frank had gotten up early and caught a couple of fish from the nearby River Little Ouse, and then cooked them over a campfire for their breakfast. Amy, having slept in, no doubt exhausted after all of last night's exertions, had only woken up just as the fish was done.
The two of them had both eagerly devoured the breakfast he had cooked, and then Amy had watched as Frank packed up their camp.
Not long after, the pair of them had set out on a lengthy hike through the woods. And all had gone well, right up until they reached the clearing...
They had found themselves approaching a large break in the trees, but neither of them could ever have anticipated what they'd find when they got there – for the scene that awaited them was like something out of a nightmare.
There seemed to be the remains of some kind of structure in the clearing, the ruined walls of some kind of ancient building, an old, abandoned church or some such and in the centre, some kind of crudely built altar, on top of which sat the severed head of a stag.
Blood and entrails littered the ground all around them, almost as though something, some poor, innocent creature - presumably the stag - had, quite literally, been ripped apart and its insides scattered all about the clearing, and the smell of death hung heavy in the air.
"What...what is all this?" Amy asked, as she followed closely behind Frank, slowly entering the clearing with him leading the way. "What...what on earth could possibly have done this?"
Amy turned and threw up into the long grass behind her – feeling nauseous and sick to her stomach at the sight of whatever it was the pair of them had happened to stumble across, out here in the forest .
"Probably some sort of an animal," Frank said, trying to sound reassuring though he didn't really believe that. He had heard whispers, over the years, of some kind of creature that was supposed to live out here in Thetford Forest – referred to locally as both The Beast of the A1075, and The Wild-man of Watton – but had always dismissed them out of hand. A few years back, someone he had worked with back at the bank had even told him the story of

their own encounter – how they had been walking through Thetford Forest one day with their dog, when the dog had become randomly and uncharacteristically spooked. Its hackles had apparently risen up, it had started to growl at nothing in particular on the trail ahead that their owner could see, and when he had gone to pick it up and carry the dog back to the car, the poor animal had been trembling with fear.

All on the journey back to the car, the dog had remained the same, and had apparently only settled down when they were finally out of the woods, but despite this, the person claimed they had never seen anything themselves that day and the next time they had taken the dog out to the forest it had been fine. There were lots of other stories told about these woods – tales of strange lights sand mysterious noises in the dead of night – but then, you could probably have said the same about any large stretch of woodland forest in Norfolk.

Hell, look at all the UFO stories people told about Rendlesham Forest.

Up until now, Frank had believed none of it – had dismissed all the stories he'd heard as simple folklore and urban legend, but now…now suddenly all those stories he recalled hearing didn't sound quite so unbelievable anymore.

"Yeah," he said, more quietly this time, almost to himself. "Probably just some kind of animal…"

He elected not to mention the scratches he could see on some of the trees that almost looked like someone, or something's, crude attempt to carve a series of ancient symbols in the bark. Amy didn't need to know about that, and right now he was more concerned with putting as much distance as he could between them and this grisly tableau that was lain out in front of them.

"We should probably go," Frank told his wife, stroking her back and holding her hair out of her face as she threw up again. "Get the hell away from here before whatever did this decides to come back…"

"You think…you think whatever did this might come back?" Amy asked, before turning back and throwing up again. In the brief second that she had faced her husband, she had felt her eyes drifting off and being drawn towards, almost against her will, something lying in the long grass behind him that had looked a lot like intestines or at the very least, something that she definitely didn't think belonged outside of a body.

"Unlikely," Frank said, doing his best to try and reassure her. "But we shouldn't take any chances, and should probably put as much distance between us and *this,* whatever *this* is, while daylight's still on our side."

Amy nodded, and allowed herself to be led round the perimeter of the clearing – well away from any more mutilated or torn apart body parts - whilst doing her level best to try and keep her eyes clear from seeing anything else nasty.

Once they were away from the clearing, Frank offered Amy a bottle of water so she could wash the taste of sick from her mouth.
"Are you okay now, hon?" he asked her, and Amy nodded.
"It was just a shock is all," she said, "seeing all that back there like that. Have…have you ever seen anything like that before?"
Frank nodded.
"Once," he said, "when I was six.
"I used to stay at my grandpa's farm every summer when I was a kid, and this one time, this fox got in the hen house and quite literally tore all the hens apart. Not for food, you understand, but just because it could.
"People may think that foxes are all cute and sweet, but in truth, they can actually be quite vicious when they want to be.
"Anyway my grandpa tracked the fox down to its lair, and then gave it the same treatment. He sent the dogs down there after the fox, its vixen, and her litter, to tear them all apart and then later, lay their bloodied bodies out around the entrance to the lair as a warning to any other foxes in the area that there were dogs about.
"He knew, you see, that the other foxes would be able to detect the smell of the dogs on the corpses and then hopefully stay away.
"I don't think I will ever forget seeing the bodies of those poor, little, baby fox cubs as they lay there, out in the woods, torn apart.
"I stopped going to my grandpa's every summer after that."
"That's a horrible story," Amy said. It was the first time he had told her about this chapter in his life, for his grandpa had been dead and long in the ground long before she had ever met her husband.
"It is what it is," Frank said. "Come on, we should probably get moving; put this whole grisly scene behind us and try and forget all about it. Let's not let this one thing ruin our whole camping trip, what do you say?"
Amy nodded.
"You're right," she said, but couldn't resist looking back one more time towards the clearing they had just passed through as they left.
The two of them shouldered their backpacks, and then continued making their way through the forest.

***

They walked late into the afternoon and early evening, stopping only once on the way for a light lunch. But the events of that morning, and the grisly scene that they had stumbled across, marred their journey.
All the way, to the place Frank had decided they would stop for the night, Amy started to become paranoid and was convinced they were being followed. She

swore she thought something was pursuing them on their way through the forest - hunting them, tracking them even - and nothing Frank tried to say to her could dissuade her. For his own part, he too thought he began hearing strange sounds in the forest – the sounds of branches breaking underfoot off in the distance as though something else was out here in the woods with them, keeping progress with them – but as they walked, he tried to convince himself that was just Amy's fears rubbing off on him.

That night, when they set up camp, there was no love-making.

Instead, the two of them just cuddled up and did their best not to discuss the elephant in the room – well, tent anyway; that the macabre events of earlier that morning, in truth, had equally unsettled them both just as much as the other.

It was Amy that woke him up, in the early hours of the morning.

It was still dark outside, that's how early it was – probably about three or four in the morning, he thought.

Amy said she thought she could hear something moving around outside, moving all around their tent and the small camp they had set up, and it was this noise, she said, that had woken her up and disturbed her.

"Can…can you hear that?" she asked him.

Frank cocked his head and listened.

His blood ran cold as he realised there was, in fact, something moving around out there – this time, at least, it wasn't just Amy's imagination and paranoia. Whatever it was, he thought, was big too from the sound of it – though for the minute, whatever it was seemed content to just continue circling their camp rather than posing either of them any threat.

Still Frank pulled Amy closer, and reached under his sleeping bag for the sheaf knife that he always kept close to him at all times, whenever they were out here in the woods.

"Shush," he whispered to her. "Try not to make any sound. Whatever it is out there, it's probably just curious is all. If we don't disturb it, maybe it will just go away…"

"But…but what is it?" Amy asked. "What do you think is out there?"

"I don't know," Frank answered, still keeping his voice down low. "A cougar maybe, possibly a bear? There have been a few lone sightings of big cats roaming out here over the years, but nothing ever actually confirmed – along with the odd sighting now and again of something some people have thought might be a bear. But they're just stories – nothing has ever been officially proven."

"Great," Amy muttered. "And you're only *now* telling me this?"

She elbowed him hard in the ribs. "Not until now, I mean. You take me out camping, tell me it's going to help me relax, and be all peaceful and shit, and

now you're telling me I'm probably going to end up getting mauled to death by a bear. Great. Thanks a lot, husband."
There was the sharp snap of a branch right outside their tent, and Amy promptly shut up quickly.
Whatever it was that was out there growled; a deep, throaty sound that echoed through the stillness of the night sending a chill through them both.
The same something, whatever it was out there, then proceeded to shake the outside of their tent, violently, as it then growled again.
"Oh God, oh God, oh God, oh God, oh God…" Amy whimpered, and even Frank felt his bladder threatening to let go. Somehow he managed to keep a hold of himself though and a second later, there was the sound of whatever had been outside their tent slowly moving away.
The creature – be it a bear, some kind of big cat, whatever – let out a howl and from the distance, there came the sound of an echoing cry as though something else out there appeared to be answering it.
Then whatever it was that had been out there was gone.
Frank and Amy held each other for a second more, and then let go.
"I…I think I just peed myself a little," Amy confessed, then let out a little hysterical laugh. Frank smiled, knowing it was just the shock of relief after what felt like a narrow escape from danger that had caused her to laugh,
 and let out a little chuckle himself.
"You know, I think I might have too," he told her in all seriousness.
Amy's voice took on a more serious tone as the reality of what had just happened started to sink in.
"Do…do you think it's really gone?" she asked.
"Only one way to find out," he told her.
Frank started to move towards the entrance to the tent.
"Don't…please…just don't," Amy whispered. "I don't want you to. Stay here with me…please."
"It's okay," Frank told her. "We heard it leave. Whatever it was out there has gone…"
"I don't care," Amy said, "I don't want you to go out there. Stay here with me."
From the tone of her voice, Frank could tell she was feeling vulnerable – and to be honest, he thought, who could blame her? They'd both just had a fright, but it had obviously affected her much more than it had him.
"Fine," Frank eventually, reluctantly, agreed. "I'll stay here."
The two of them cuddled up, and it was not long before they both went back to sleep.
Whilst outside, in the darkness, something stood there and watched them…and waited…

***

Sometime during the night, while they were still asleep, it must have rained, and rained heavily for when they awoke, there was no sign of any tracks, nor any other indication that their campsite had been visited in the dead of night.

If they hadn't both experienced the same thing, Frank thought, then he might even have put last night's little visit down to a bad dream.

But it had happened.

There was no denying it now.

Something was out here in the woods with them.

As they cooked breakfast, the two of them discussed heading back to the car and cutting their camping trip short.

Frank knew exactly where they were, and knew it would only take another hour or so from here to get back to where they'd parked the car, as they had kind of come around in a big circle. They had been intending to leave sometime late tomorrow anyway, so wouldn't be cutting their trip short by much and besides, neither of them thought they could relax now knowing that whatever it was that had visited them last night was still out there somewhere, and might well come back again tonight.

"It's up to you," Frank told Amy as they ate. "What do you think?"

"I don't want to go," Amy admitted, "but at the same time, what if we move on, set up camp somewhere else and whatever it was last night *does* come back? Finds us again? What if it thinks we've invaded its territory or something, and last night was just meant as some kind of warning to warn us off?"

"I very much doubt we'll see whatever it was again," Frank said. "But if nothing else, we should probably alert the Forestry Commission as soon as we get back. Tell them we think we heard something out here. I mean, with no proof and the fact we never saw anything, they probably won't do anything or take us too seriously, but I do think it's kind of our duty to warn them *something* might be out here that might possibly pose a threat to other campers."

In the end, Frank and Amy agreed not to let last night's experience ruin the rest of their day, but also agreed it was probably in both their best interests to leave before nightfall and go home a day early. Camped as they were, not far from the River Little Ouse, Frank now pulled out the inflatable kayak they had brought with them, and began the slow process of pumping it up so they could get in a little bit of canoeing before it became time for them to pack up their stuff, head back to their car and from there, drive the short journey home.

Once he was done, Amy helped him guide the small boat out into the river.

Out on the water, everything was still.

At this time of year there was a cool and refreshing breeze, but it barely seemed to touch the river and as they rowed, Frank contemplated how it was actually quite peaceful and serene out here - miles away from civilisation or any other form of life - and found himself almost regretting the decision they had both made for them to leave their long weekend away early.

He was just about to turn to Amy and ask her whether she thought they should maybe reconsider leaving later, and stay another day after all, when Amy suddenly spoke up and said she'd spotted something – watching them from the opposite bank.

"Look, over there – do you see it?" she demanded, as Frank slowly brought their kayak to a halt in the water. "Over there, in the woods…something's definitely watching us!"

Frank looked over to where he thought Amy was pointing.

For a moment he could not see anything, but then he suddenly saw it.

A tall, dark, what looked like hairy figure…standing there, watching them from amongst the trees directly opposite from where they had stopped in the water. As Frank watched, the figure turned around and walked back off into the undergrowth until it was lost from sight.

"What…what was that?" Amy asked, a level of panic evident in her voice. "Was that…do you think…was that the *thing* from last night, do you think?"

"I don't think so," Frank said, doing his best to try and reassure her. "I only caught a glimpse, no more than that," he lied.

"I mean, it could have been anything…*anyone*, I mean," he said quickly, correcting himself. "Probably just a Forest Ranger…or maybe somebody living out here in the woods. You know, like some kind of homeless guy or Wild-man or something…you do hear about these things. Hell, maybe that was who visited us last night – some kind of local living out here in the forest who maybe just wanted to scare us off."

He was making things up now in a bid to try and calm her, but he didn't think she was buying it and even Frank didn't think he sounded all that convincing, even in his *own* head.

"Can we turn back?" Amy asked. "I'm sorry, Frank. Can we just turn around and row back now. Please? I don't feel safe out here anymore…not with that *thing* out there watching us, whatever it was. Maybe you're right, maybe it is just someone living out here rough trying to scare us, but I'd be a lot happier if we just turned round and headed back to camp.

"Please, Frank. Pretty please."

There was a whiney sound to her voice now and reluctantly, Frank agreed to turn the small kayak they were in around.

It was never pretty to hear her beg – not her or *any* woman in fact, he thought, and decided it was probably in his best interests to just do what she wanted or he would only end up paying the price for it afterwards.
"Okay, okay, we'll head back," he said eventually, and sighed. "But you do know we've barely been out here in the water for less than an hour?"
"I just think I'll feel a lot safer if we just head back and start the long walk back to the car is all," Amy said, instantly scuppering any further discussion Frank might have been contemplating about staying out here for the extra day that they had planned.
Frank turned the boat around and rowed them back to the place where they had set up camp last night.
And that's when everything took an even bigger turn for the worse…

***

As soon as they reached the bank, Frank could see something was wrong. The small camp that they had so meticulously set up last night was now in absolute ruin and disarray.
Their bags that they'd brought with them had all been opened, and their possessions scattered about, and their tent had been ripped and torn, presumably by some animal's claws or talons, and was now threatening to be blown away at any minute by the light breeze coming off the water.
More than that, whatever it was that had visited their camp while they were away had also obviously torn apart some kind of small animal or rodent whilst it was there, for bits of entrails and ripped apart internal organs quite literally covered their whole camp. Frank could see what he assumed were bits of some small animal's intestines, and pieces of its guts, hanging from the trees and littering the ground all around their tent; presumably, he thought, from some kind of small rodent or rabbit for on closer inspection, whatever had done this had ripped off the poor animal's head and staked it in the ground, on a large branch, right outside the entrance to their tent.
Amy gasped when she saw the damage, and then gripped him ever more tightly, in blind panic and outright fear, when she saw the pieces of the dead animal scattered all around their small camp.
Frank took her head and turned it into his shoulder so as to help her avoid from seeing the poor, decapitated rabbit, but from her shaking and sobbing in his arms, thought it might already be too late.
Now, any thoughts he'd ever entertained about possibly staying another night out here were well and truly off the table, he thought. Whatever had done this had to be the same creature that had visited them in the wee hours last night, he

told himself, and maybe even the same thing that had been watching them out on the water.

It would be certain madness to stay out here now, Frank told himself.

From the look of it, and the similarity of this grisly scene in front of them to that they had accidentally stumbled across yesterday morning, when they had first set out, Frank thought, they had obviously unintentionally somehow crossed over into what some creature considered as its hunting ground, and this was obviously its way of assuming dominance and warning them off.

To stay out here after all this, Frank thought, would be nothing less than foolhardy – suicide even. They needed to go, and right now, but more than that, much more, they definitely needed to alert the Forestry Commission now because whatever it was that was out here, Frank thought, there was no longer any question it posed a very real threat not just to them, but also to anyone else who came out here.

"Oh Frank, Frank," Amy sobbed, her voice muffled by the thick coat he was wearing as she spoke into his shoulder. "What...what could have done this? We need to get out of here ...and *now*...I mean it, Frank. I'm...*we're*...not staying here any longer. We need to get out of here – and preferably before whatever did this comes back!"

She was echoing his exact same thoughts, Frank thought. There was still plenty of time before nightfall, more than half a day in fact, and Frank thought he still had a pretty good idea in which direction their car was parked.

If they headed off now, they could easily make it back there and get back on the road before darkness, Frank thought, and then they could put all of all this far behind them.

Some kind of relaxing getaway this turned out to be, he thought to himself, then motioned Amy to stay here by the kayak.

"Stay here," he told her, "and don't look. I'll clear up as best I can, pack up whatever's left of our stuff that hasn't already been ruined, and we'll get straight out of here, I promise. Okay? We'll be back at the car, and back on the road, before you know it, I swear, and then we can just forget all about all this and pretend like it never happened, okay?"

Amy nodded.

She was sobbing, he noted. The tears quite literally pouring down her face. The last time he had seen her this scared, he thought, was when she had been at the hospital and had finally acknowledged that she had lost the baby.

Her first thoughts back then had been of him – that he would leave her because she was barren and could not bear him what he had always wanted, a child - but he had told her then, in that moment, and had meant it, that he would never leave her side.

For better or for worse, he had reminded her.

True, the last eighteen months or so since the miscarriage had been hard, and physical contact – let alone sex – between them had been scarce and pretty much off the table, but she was still his wife and he had made a commitment to her on their wedding day that he fully intended to keep.

Not just to stay with her, he thought, but also to keep her safe.

"Stay here," he told her now, repeating himself, not sure if she had really heard him the first time in her shock at the sight before them. "Wait here, I'll go pack up our stuff, what's left of it, and then we can clear the hell out of here."

He left her to start packing up, trying to avoid looking at the grisly remains scattered all around their camp.

The rabbit's head, he gently removed from the stake, and then turned it around as he lay it in the grass, so it's dead, lifeless eyes could no longer stare right back at him.

That was the one thing that had probably disturbed him the most, he thought. For the head had obviously been left there as warning, to provoke some kind of reaction or response, and was a sign that their camp had obviously been visited by something of rudimentary intelligence at the very least...

And not just some dumb animal.

It was only as he went to pack away what remained of their tent, and the sleeping bags that lay therein, that he realised that they were wet – and then realised why. Both the tent and their sleeping bags were soaked through with urine – a sure indication that whatever it was that had visited their camp while they'd been away, had done so with the express motive of marking its territory.

Frank decided to leave whatever else he had not packed up already – it was long past time, he thought, that they got the hell out of here.

After all of it was all only…stuff.

It was much more important right now, he thought, that they get out of here with their lives.

Amy had not yet deflated the kayak and Frank was glad of that.

"Get in," he told her now. "We need to get away, leave, get out of here right now, and if we kayak down the river aways, we'll have less further to walk and it'll take us a whole lot less time to get back to the car."

There was a level of fear to his tone and Amy, not stupid by any means, could hear it in his voice the moment that he spoke.

"What is it?" she asked. "What happened? What's changed? What have you seen?"

"I don't want to talk about it right now, alright?" he said. "Let's just go, get in the boat and go."

"But…but, Frank…what…" she said again, but Frank shut her down.

"I mean it," he said. "You were right, let's just get the hell out of here, okay?" He pushed the kayak away from the shore.
A minute later, they were well on their way...

***

Frank had estimated it would take them both about one and a half to two hours to walk back to the car. By kayaking partway down the river, they managed to cut that time in half.
As they hiked back in the direction Frank knew the car to be - after coming back to shore several miles away, back down the river - both of them were silent.
As well as listening and keeping an ear out for any sign of pursuit, the pair of them were trying to avoid going over old ground again.
There was no point discussing what may or may not be hunting them, or what they had seen, or what may have visited them in the early hours of last night back at their camp, for they had no way of knowing what it was and there really was no point speculating.
And that was the way he wanted to try and keep it, Frank thought. He was happy enough not knowing, and would be happier still when they finally arrived back home and were many, many miles away from here.
He did not mind not knowing.
He actually preferred the mystery.
After all, what was it they said about ignorance being bliss?
He was scared enough already, and knew that Amy was as well, and didn't need to know what was hunting them – his main priority right now was just somehow getting through all of this, and managing to survive long enough to escape these damned fucking woods.
If this were a horror movie, he couldn't help thinking as they walked, *then when they arrived at the car, it would be trashed by whatever it was that was out here with them.* Thankfully, when they eventually arrived at the car, everything was fine and the vehicle looked exactly as they'd left it.
We'll get in, and then it won't start, Frank thought, as he opened up the back and stowed what little remained of the stuff they'd brought with them inside. *The battery will be flat, and then we'll be stuck out here, and forced to try and walk out of here...*
But when they both climbed in and Frank started up the engine, the car started up first time.
The road will be blocked, he thought. *We'll get halfway down the track, and then that thing back there will have somehow managed to get in front of us and will have blocked the only way out of here with a fallen tree or something...*

But as Frank began to drive, taking it slow and easy down the back country trail that would eventually lead them out of Thetford Forest and back onto the main road, this too soon proved false.
Gaining confidence now, and much more positive that they were actually going to make it out of these woods alive, Frank started to speed up…and that was when something rushed out onto the trail in front of him.
Frank slammed his foot down on the brakes, and the car instantly ground to a halt – throwing both him and Amy forward as it impacted with whatever was in front of them. Dazed and confused, Frank barely registered the creature bringing down both its hands upon the bonnet, smashing the engine in anger and essentially trashing their only viable way out of here, before another blur of movement, rushing towards them, coming from his right, momentarily distracted him.
As he turned to look out of the side window, the thing rushing towards them on the driver's side collided with them, hard, – forcing them off the road as their vehicle first flipped over, and then rolled, and then promptly carried on rolling down a sharp, steep ditch by the side of the road.
With each new impact, Frank struck his head and from somewhere close by, he could hear his wife, Amy, continually screaming hysterically as the car flipped over and over and over on its way down the steep embankment.
Only their seatbelts prevented them from being thrown out of the car.
A second later, as they reached the bottom, there was one last and final impact…and then everything all went black.

***

When Frank finally came to, he awoke to discover himself being dragged through the forest by his feet. Every last bit of him hurt, and ached, no doubt from where he had been bounced around in his car when it had fallen down that ditch, and he had a headache fit to burst that he was certain was a sure sign of concussion.
He tried to crane his neck, and lift his head, from where he was being pulled along the forest floor, so he could try and see who or what was dragging him, or at the very least try and catch a glimpse of Amy in case she might be close by, but he couldn't. The back of his neck was too stiff, presumably from whiplash, and all he could see in front of him of his captor was something or someone big, impossibly tall, and hairy like some kind of primitive caveman or, worst case scenario, some kind of Sasquatch or Bigfoot.
But that was just ridiculous, right
The stories about Bigfoot, or Sasquatch, living out here in these woods were all just stories, right?

They couldn't possibly be true.
Except apparently, he thought, they were.
As he thought about everything that had happened to them the last few days, Frank felt himself starting to panic.
At the very least if his kidnapper were human, he thought, then he might stand some small, slim chance of trying to reason with his captor.
But if his kidnapper, on the other hand, was some kind of savage beast…like a Sasquatch or a Bigfoot like the local urban legends would suggest lived out here…well then suddenly, he thought, his odds of survival seemed a lot less likely.
He had to try and get them both away from here, he thought.
He and Amy both.
At the very least, he needed to try and ensure Amy somehow managed to escape, even if that meant sacrificing his own life to make that happen.
Amy, he thought suddenly.
He still didn't know what had happened to his wife…was she even actually still here with him now?
Or had whatever it was that had hold of him left her back there at the car?
"Amy," he tried to call out, but his voice came out as no more than a croak.
"Amy," he tried again. "Can you hear me, Amy? Amy? AMY…" but t silence was the only reply.
If she *was* out here with him, he thought, being dragged along like him by her ankles, then she was probably still out cold just like he had been up until a few minutes ago. Either that or she was dead, and that was something Frank really didn't want to think about or even consider right now.
Because if she were dead, then that left him with no reason to go on…
As he strained to try and look up again, or at least try and see where he was being taken, he saw he was being pulled towards some kind of great, big, massive fissure in the ground. A hole leading into what looked like some kind of massive great tunnel, headed underground, that almost looked like it had been dug out of the earth like a rabbit warren, and that was partially hidden from casual sight by the roots of a fallen tree.
As he and his captor drew closer and closer to their destination, Frank reached out in a vain attempt to try and grab something that might possibly halt his progress – a tree root or something, anything – but to no avail.
"Amy," he tried to call out again, his voice still no more than a hoarse whisper. "Amy, are you there?"
Then suddenly Frank's head struck something protruding from the ground, some kind of rock or something, and the next thing he knew, everything went black once more.

***

When he awoke for the second time, Frank was being dragged down some kind of tunnel – presumably the same one he had been headed towards earlier before he had struck his head. He could still see no sign of Amy, but at least this time he could hear her – whimpering, crying and sobbing somewhere close by him as she pleaded for her life, even as the two of them were dragged ever further and further, deeper beneath the ground.
"Amy," he called out, this time much louder than before, "AMY, AMY…" and as he heard his voice echo around the walls of the tunnel, at least this time he actually got a response.
"Frank…Frank…oh my God, is that you? What happened to us…where…where are we? What's going on? Where are we being taken?"
Amy's voice sounded scared, terrified in fact, and Frank did his best to try and reassure her.
"Amy, stay calm. It'll all be okay, I promise you," Frank called back, trying to sound braver than he actually felt with a false sense of bravado and confidence. Even though he could not see where she was, he was confident she was close – just behind him maybe, or possibly somewhere in front of him.
At least, he thought, now he knew that she was still alive…
"Everything's going to be alright, I promise. We're going to get out of this. I promise you."
The creature who was dragging him stopped for a second, there in the tunnel, and turned to face him. Frank just had a glimpse of an angry, snarling face, there in the darkness before him, and then the creature, whatever it was, lashed out with a massive, hairy fist to silence him, hitting him hard in the face.
The last thing Frank heard was Amy calling his name, then once again everything went black…

***

When he woke up for the third and final time, Frank was suspended upside down. He appeared to be in some kind of cavern, with a small campfire burning in the centre providing the only illumination – the smoke being pulled upwards towards a hole in the ceiling; a natural vent that seemed to be acting like some kind of chimney.
He had no idea where he was, or how far underground he might be, but guessed this must be where that creature that had been dragging him all this time had ultimately been taking him. He could still hear Amy somewhere - close behind, he thought, though the acoustics down here made it difficult to tell - but just as before, he could not see her. He could just hear her sobbing somewhere off in the darkness, hidden from him by the shadows.

"Amy…Amy…" he called out, but wasn't sure how close she was or even if she could hear him. "Get the hell away from her. Keep your filthy hands off her, you bastards!"
Something moved in front of him.
Something massive, well-built, and extremely hairy.
As Frank hung there upside down, helpless, suspended from the ceiling by some kind of rope or vine, the creature in front of him bent down and tilted its face to look at him and for the first time, Frank got a good, hard look at the beast that had abducted him.
It was like something out of a nightmare.
The creature stood back upright and in a single movement, lashed out with its claws, opening up Frank's stomach with its razor-sharp talons, sending his insides tumbling out onto the floor.
As the rest of the Bigfoot that had been surrounding him all this time, hidden by the darkness of the cavern, slowly started to emerge from where they had been waiting, the creatures closed in on him and began to feed.
The last thing Frank heard, just before he died, was the sound of Amy screaming, somewhere close behind him.
Her screams were the last sound he would ever get to hear…

Two

Frank and Amy Hayden were not reported missing for another five days and when they eventually were, local authorities spent the next three weeks scouring the length and breadth of Thetford Forest, searching for any sign of them, but all to no avail.
 Other than the wreckage of the pair's vehicle, there appeared to be no other indication as to what might have happened to them, or where they might have gone and so, after an extensive ad campaign and a nationwide appeal for any information that likewise proved fruitless, eventually the authorities ended up deciding enough was enough.
And with no sign of the couple, they gave up and called off the search.
All except for one man.
Detective Inspector Chris Jennings.
D.I. Jennings was convinced Frank and Amy Hayden were still out there somewhere, deep in the heart of Thetford Forest and what was more, he believed that he knew what might have happened to them.
Ever since his own experience in the forest over two decades before, D.I. Jennings had become obsessed with anything and everything related to The

Bigfoot of Thetford Forest - otherwise known as The Wild-man of Watton, or sometimes The Beast of the A1075, because of the locations where it had always been sighted. And over the years, despite there being very few actual confirmed sightings, Chris Jennings had gathered together quite an extensive file full of uncorroborated reports and alleged eye witness accounts related to this local urban legend, and had even tracked several mysterious disappearances down to the same area of the forest that he had come to refer to as 'The Thetford Triangle'.

His friends and colleagues all thought he was nuts, and a bit of an obsessive - and called him, 'The Monster Hunter' both behind his back *and* to his face - and it was partly because of this that when he had gone to his superiors with his theories that Frank and Amy's disappearances might be linked to several others that had all gone missing in this alleged 'Triangle' of his, they had immediately dismissed him out of hand.

The local authorities had searched *everywhere* in the forest, they told him, and had found precisely nothing. What made him think, they asked, that by going out there he would find anything that they hadn't?

They neglected to mention that many of the search dogs had become agitated during the search and that afterwards, many of them – despite being well-trained with years of experience working as both cadaver and search and rescue dogs – had refused to re-enter the forest, but D.I Jennings knew people, and had spoken to many of the search parties involved, and the stories they'd told him had only served to confirm his own suspicions.

There was something out there, living in the heart of Thetford Forest, Jennings thought, and whatever it was, it was more than likely the same thing responsible for the mysterious disappearance of Frank and Amy Hayden.

And so, one day, almost two months to the date Frank and Amy had first disappeared, D.I. Chris Jennings finally decided to take matters into his own hand. He had announced that he was taking some annual leave, had gone home and packed, and then he had headed out here.

Out to Thetford Forest…

***

It wasn't just Bigfoot.

D.I Chris Jennings was obsessed with all things cryptozoological, especially if it was Norfolk-related and over the years, had spent time on Pentney Lakes looking for the alleged monster supposed to be hiding in its depths, and wandered the Fens searching for any sign of Black Shuck or the big cats also supposed to be living out there.

But up until now, all his investigations had turned up nothing.

This time though, Jennings thought, this time he was going to be proven right, he was sure of it, and then, just for once, he would be able to go back to his superiors and it would be *he* who would be the one laughing last.

He had gathered all the information he could on Frank and Amy, marked out on a map of the forest the trails he thought were the most likely they might have used, and intended to follow in their footsteps as close to the route he thought they must have taken as possible.

The official story the authorities had released was that Frank and Amy must have swerved off the road to avoid a deer or something on their way back out of the forest, and that was how their car had ended up in the ditch. Dazed and concussed, the theory was that they then must have left their vehicle and become lost in the forest trying to find their way out.

But as strong as this theory was, it failed to explain where they might be now; what might have happened to the couple after their crash;, or offer up any kind of explanation as to why in the weeks that followed, not a single trace of them had been found.

It also failed to explain why only half their camping equipment and gear had been found in what remained of their car.

No tents had been found, and no sleeping bags.

Authorities from the Forestry Commission had claimed this was a clear sign and indication that Frank and Amy had still been alive and clear-headed when they left the car. That they had taken the camping gear with them when they left, and that the couple would inevitably turn up in another few weeks or so, dehydrated and hungry from where they had simply gotten lost.

But it didn't explain why they had taken only half of their stuff, leaving all the rest, and had only taken their sleeping bags and tent and nothing else.

Now, as Jennings reached the point where the Frank and Amy's car had been found, he pulled out his map and consulted it.

Further along was the place where the Forest Rangers had theorised the couple had originally parked their car, according to tire tracks they had found, and from there, there were only a couple of routes Frank and Amy possibly could have taken unless they wanted to go cross-country through thick trees and bush.

But that would just have been stupid and from all Jennings had read about the couple, they hadn't been stupid.

Carefully, he unshouldered the rifle he had brought with him for protection, and then reaching in the side-pocket of his backpack for a small, hand-held video camera, opened it up and turning it to face him, started to record.

As part of his search, Jennings intended to document all of his findings and then, if he did see something out here – be it Bigfoot, a bear, or something else entirely – at least then he would have some sort of physical proof of what he'd seen or in the very worst case scenario, would have left behind some kind of record for others to find, just in case anything *did* happen to him out here in the Forest.

No way did Jennings intend to become just another statistic like Frank and Amy Hayden - just one more mysterious disappearance in the so-called 'Thetford Triangle' he had uncovered that, to his best estimation, had been responsible for at least a half a dozen people going missing in the last twenty years or so, and those were just the ones that had been reported.

It wasn't just disappearances that happened out here though, he thought.

Over the last couple of decades of looking into the forest, Jennings had also found reports of a number of alleged suicides had also occurred out here – alleged because of those who had supposedly come out here to die, none of them had shown any previous history of depression or even any indication of suicidal thoughts before they had come out here to kill themselves.

The most recent incident had occurred just last year.

An esteemed local physician who had come out here to the forest supposedly to indulge in a bit of camping under the stars, along with a bit of hunting and fishing, had been found about a week later by some hikers, hanging from a tree. All of his colleagues, and all those who had worked closely with him up at the Norfolk and Norwich hospital over the years, had all been in agreement that his taking his own life had been totally out of character, but on the surface at least, the evidence had seemed to speak for itself.

The only troubling thing had been the doctor's failure to leave any kind of a suicide note, but as D.I Jennings knew from all his past years of experience on the force, that was not always any indication that a death was suspicious.

People did not always leave suicide notes when they chose to end their life, and certainly not as frequently or often as they did in books and on the telly - for if they were thinking clearly enough to leave a note, in the majority of cases that often meant they were not ready to die and that their suicide attempt had been no more of a plea for help.

When the hikers had found the man's body, there had already been signs that some kind of animal had been feeding on him, for his belly had been ripped open and many of his insides were missing. But this, in itself, would not have been unusual if the body had been there for several days as the evidence would suggest…except for one little thing.

Jennings had spoken to the coroner who had autopsied the body, his interest piqued by the location in which the doctor's corpse had been found, and had been told, unofficially and off the record, that it was of the coroner's opinion that whatever animal it was that had fed on him, it appeared to have done so while the late doctor was still alive…

The Coroner had not had enough evidence to confirm this, he'd told Jennings at the time, and in the end, under advice, had ended up electing to leave it out of the official autopsy report in order to spare the immediate family any more grief, but he had sworn to Jennings that he hadn't been mistaken, and that had been more than enough for the Detective.

Which was why, today, he'd brought the gun out here with him.

As Jennings spun the camera to face himself, he spoke into the tiny microphone.

"Day One of my unofficial search for the missing campers, Frank and Amy Hayden," he said, keeping his voice loud and clear so it could be easily picked up by the cheap camera – all he could afford on his wages.

"I'm here, in Thetford Forest, at the site where Frank and Amy Hayden's 4x4 was found, abandoned, after it had presumably been involved in some kind of incident that sent it crashing down into this ditch. Obviously the car is long gone now, taken away by the authorities, but when it was first found, fresh traces of blood along with traces of the couple's DNA were discovered inside the vehicle, indicating they were most likely the only people inside when the vehicle was sent careening down into this gully for whatever reason. Did the couple strike something on the trail, a deer perhaps? Or did they lose control and just swerve off the road? Unless we find either of them alive, it is doubtful we will ever know, but according to official reports there did appear to be some damage sustained to the vehicle not consistent with the car rolling down into this ditch, suggesting they may have collided with someone or something in the moments just before they were sent crashing down to the bottom of this steep slope that you can see behind me."

Jennings spun the camera around 90 degrees so that he could document the slope the Hayden's car had fallen down.

"What might have happened to Frank and Amy Hayden after that, and where they might have wandered off too, remains a mystery and right now, is impossible to say, but that is what I intend to try and discover over the course of the next few days.

"I *do* have a theory, and think I might well have an *idea* what might possibly have happened to them, but proving it, however, will be another matter entirely.

"And so begins my search for the truth behind the disappearance of Frank and Amy Hayden and along the way, who knows, possibly even the creature known as 'The Bigfoot of Thetford Forest' as well."

D.I Chris Jennings finished filming, put the video camera back in his backpack, and then shouldering his rifle once more started to move off down the most likely route he estimated Frank and Amy must have gone that first day they had come out here. He had no way of knowing for certain it was the direction they

might have gone, but after studying their previous trips out here, thought it was an educated guess.
From deep within the woods, unseen, someone or *something*, watched him go...

Three

Just as when Frank and Amy had set out over two months ago, Detective Jennings's first day out in Thetford Forest was largely uneventful.
He had no problem finding the place where searchers thought the couple must have set up camp that first night - for there was still evidence of some kind of campfire even now, months later and at this time of year, visitors to this part of the forest, other than by the Forestry Commission, were few and far between - and so made the decision to set up his own tent very close to the same area.
Jennings's tent was only a small one – barely even a one-man tent – and heavily camouflaged already, but once it was set up away from the main clearing where it was assumed Frank and Amy had spent their first night, the Detective used broken branches and bits of fallen leaves to help make it even less visible unless you knew exactly what it was you were looking for.
This done, he quickly donned the ghillie suit he had brought with him, that he had purchased from a stall on Skegness market a few years ago now, and then retired to the tent that he intended to use tonight as a hide, to spy on anything that might come sniffing around in the middle of the night.
The ghillie suit he was wearing was based on standard army-issue, and designed to replicate the camouflage suits that snipers often wore, whilst out on missions, to help them avoid detection and blend in with their background. This particular suit he was wearing was made up of several pieces of overlapping burlap material made to resemble twigs and branches, foliage and leaves, and his hope was that out here in the forest, it would aid him in hunting down whatever it was that might be out here.
His suit donned, Jennings finally lay back in his tent and prepared to catch a few z's. He had already set up his small video-camera at the entrance of his tent, and switched it to motion-sensitive mode so it would only activate and start recording if it sensed any movement.
He did not fully expect to see anything on his first night out here, but if anything *did* come by, then he definitely wanted to catch it on camera. He wanted to be the first person to catch whatever it was that lived out here in Thetford Forest, in the same way that Patterson and Gimlin had historically been the first to capture the American Bigfoot on film.

Their footage had become legendary over time, and Jennings was kind of hoping that before he left in a few days, as well as solving the mystery of what might have happened to Frank and Amy Hayden, he might also walk away with his own empirical evidence of whatever it was that lived out here in Thetford forest.

It was also his security - so if the same thing happened to him as he strongly believed might have happened to Frank and Amy Hayden, then there might be be some sort of record left behind to show what might have befallen him.

It was not yet full dark outside, and dusk was only just falling, but here, deep in the heart of the forest, it looked much darker than it actually was because of the large number of trees surrounding him, cutting off what little remained of the natural light. Jennings set his watch to wake him up in a few hours when full-dark finally set in, closed his eyes, and prepared to drift off to sleep so he could catch forty winks.

He had come out here to solve a mystery, he thought, not become one himself, and one way or another he was determined not to leave here without first gaining some answers.

***

At a little over 19,000 hectares, and around 47,000 acres, Thetford Forest was the largest lowland pine forest in Britain and one of only a handful of Sites of Special Scientific Interest throughout the whole of the United Kingdom. Not just because of the wide variety of rare flora and fauna that grew there, but also because the forest was home to several rare species of breeding birds such as Woodlarks, Nightjars, Goshawks and Crossbills.

It was also home to a large population of hares, rabbits and several species of deer, amongst them Muntjac, Roe deer and a small number of Red deer.

But Thetford Forest was a man-made forest, not a natural one.

It had been created after the First World War to help provide a strategic reserve of timber after all the demands of the war, and it was because of this that many people thought there was no possible way it could be home to anything as mysterious as Bigfoot - for if such creatures did exist, then surely by now some sort of evidence would have turned up to prove their existence.

Those people were wrong…as Detective Chris Jennings was soon about to find out.

***

Detective Jennings woke up sometime much later, only to find darkness had already fallen. Checking his watch, he saw that he had obviously slept through all of his alarms, because several hours had already passed and it was now extremely late in the evening. No doubt all the hiking he had done that day, coupled with all the fresh, country air, must have rendered him more tired than he'd realised, he thought.

At first, as Jennings lay there, alone in the darkness, he was unsure what must have woken him, but then he heard it...the sound of something large, and cumbersome, moving, out there in the forest, somewhere just outside his tent.

Bigfoot, he thought. *It just had to be...*

There was no reason for him to think this - for in truth, if he were being honest with himself, whatever it was that was out there might just as likely be a deer or some other nocturnal animal – but somehow he didn't think so.

No, whatever it was, it sounded much too large to be a deer.

The rational part of his mind argued against this – tried to tell him that at night, with the silence of the forest all around, often noises seemed much louder than they actually were – but the irrational part of his mind continued to argue otherwise.

No, it was Bigfoot out there, he thought.

He didn't know how he knew that, he just did...

Moving as quietly as he could to the front of his tent, Jennings kneeled by his camera and saw straight away that it had already started recording, confirming that something was definitely moving around out there in the forest.

He had already set the camera to night-vision mode before he'd dozed off and gone to sleep and now, as he put his eye to the lens, he looked to see what might possibly have set it recording, a wave of disappointment was sent crashing through him.

A deer, he thought. *It was just a deer.*

An impressive stag to be fair, and a mighty sight to behold, but still just a deer nonetheless.

He was just about to turn away from the camera, when something massive rose up from the tree-line behind it. Effortlessly and silently, the creature, whatever it was - and was there any question, it had to be Bigfoot this time, surely – grabbed the majestic deer by the throat and lifting the poor, innocent creature up on its hind legs, promptly proceeded to snap its neck like a twig with an audible crack, before the poor animal could even think about fleeing or attempting to escape.

"*Fu...*" Jennings started to say, then remembering how far sound travelled at night, promptly cut himself off before he could finish that thought. Even though he'd only spoken in the quietest of whispers the Bigfoot though, if that was indeed what it was, must have heard something, for as Jennings watched, the beast turned its head and seemed to stare directly towards him for a moment in the direction of him and his camera.

Opening up its maw, the creature let out a deafening roar; so loud, Jennings thought he could feel the very earth around him vibrating. From further off, deeper in the forest, came an answering roar – then another one…
There were more of them out there than the one stood there before him, Frank suddenly realised, and they were close, he thought. A bit too frighteningly close.
A little too close for comfort…
Jennings froze where he was, his blood slowly turning to ice and a cold chill running through his bones. Keeping his movements slow, and steady, he started to reach behind him for his gun – just in case, you understand, just as a precaution; just on the off-chance the beast *did* decide to attack - but for some reason the darn thing kept evading his grasp. Still Jennings kept trying, for even though he knew chances were he was safe, sitting here camouflaged as he was in his tent, he knew that situation might change at any moment.
The slightest movement, the slightest sound, he thought, at any minute might give him away and then, he thought, all bets were off…
As the beast opened up its mighty jaw and once let out another roar, Jennings gave up trying to reach for his gun and once more froze where he was.
Feeling his bladder let go, Jennings thought he felt himself piss himself a little, and didn't think he'd ever felt as terrified in his whole, entire life before as he was currently feeling right now.
Then just like that, the Bigfoot turned around and without further ado, headed off back into the forest, back the way it had come, dragging the dead deer behind it.
Jennings let out a small sigh of relief.
That was close, he thought. *Too darn close for his liking…but at least he now had the evidence he'd sought after. Now, at least, he could prove there really was something out here.*
Now all that remained was to discover the truth behind what might have happened to Frank and Amy Hayden, he thought. If he could uncover their bones, find evidence of their passing, it would prove, beyond all reasonable shadow of a doubt, that he had been right all along what had happened to them. It was a hell of a risk, he thought, but a calculated one – the video footage on its own would not be enough and after all, discovering what might have happened to a Frank and Amy Hayden was the *real* reason he had come out here.
Jennings sat back in his tent and finally able to lay his hands on his rifle, pulled his gun closer towards him.
Only once he was sure that the Bigfoot was unlikely to return, did Detective Jennings finally allow himself to start to relax.
Needless to say, however, he spent the rest of the night wide awake.

Four

Professor Hilary Clarke was a noted and once well respected lecturer in the subject of Cryptozoology. Just over a year ago now, Detective Chris Jennings had paid him a visit at the Norwich and West Norfolk University that served as one of the largest campuses in the whole of East Anglia, and that had very close ties with The Greenacres Laboratory and Institute of Scientific Research.
Professor Clarke's office was located in the basement of the University and when Detective Jennings first entered the room, he was greeted by the sight of shelf after shelf crammed almost to full with dusty old books and rare and out of print texts, and walls that were all literally covered with ancient and falling apart maps of the world, that no doubt had been out-of-date and inaccurate even back when Columbus had first set sail for the New World.
Professor Hilary Clarke was everything that you might expect a typical, middle-aged, and formerly highly esteemed lecturer in Cryptozoology to be – a walking cliché as it were.
He wore a tweed jacket with patches on each elbow, a pair of glasses mended with tape that had obviously seen better days, and what was more, he smoked a pipe – indoors - even though it had long been made illegal to smoke inside, and was even more especially frowned upon at what was supposed to be an institute of supposedly advanced and higher education, that had recently been named as one of the top universities in the country.
"You must be Detective Jennings," the Professor said, when the Detective first knocked, and then entered upon invitation to do so. "So tell me, Detective – how is it I can help you today? And how is it exactly that I can be of assistance?"
"How did you know who I was?" Detective Chris Jennings asked of the man sitting in front of him, his desk likewise littered with ancient maps like those on the walls, and an impossibly high stack of old books that looked like it might topple and fall over at any minute.
"Who else might it be?" The Professor asked in return. "I mean, it's not like I get many visitors to my office nowadays – or many students wanting to take any of my lectures anymore - hence why I've been shoved down here in the basement. Many of my formerly *esteemed* colleagues," he said with a sneer and a slight air of contempt, "no longer even consider Cryptozoology to be a real subject, and I seem to have largely fallen out of favour with much of the faculty of late, but as my family have plenty of money and over the years have spent much of that money keeping this university afloat, it's not like they can just get rid of me any time soon.

"So instead, this is where they put me and in the meantime, try to forget I exist – but what they don't know is the last laugh is on me.

"Down here, I can get up to whatever I wish – I can do what I want, study what I want, even smoke down here if I want with no-one from upstairs telling me otherwise, so tell me now, who's the old fool?

"Not me, that's for sure.

"Nowadays, it's almost like Cryptozoology has become a dirty word - all students ever want to talk about and study these days is 'Environmental Science'. What's that all about, I ask you?

"Did you know, there's a Professor up there who truly believes that Global-warming and Climate Change are a result of ancient, old gods attempting to terraform the planet, ready for their eventual return like something out of Lovecraft? I mean, he *really*, truly believes that.

"You tell me, what do you think?

"Is that truly the sort of thing we should be teaching our youth nowadays?

"I don't think so, do you?

"But I'm sorry, I digress. You came here for a reason, no?"

The professor rose from his chair.

"Let me clear you some space and make you a seat, and then you can sit down and tell me how it is I can help you today. I'm assuming it is still today up there?" he asked, for needless to say there were no windows down here in the basement, which made for a very smoky environment whenever the professor lit up his pipe as he had at the moment, making it very difficult to breathe down here, what with all the dust floating around as well.

The only source of ventilation seemed to come from a series of air vents located high up in the far wall, Jennings noted, and the whole place was quite literally a firetrap. It was a wonder that the whole place hadn't all caught alight and gone up in flames already, he thought. But the way the ageing professor was puffing on his pipe, it could only be a matter of time before a stray spark started a fire amongst all these scraps of crumbling paper.

Professor Clarke came around from behind his desk and started to clear away a pile of books from a chair, that up until now had lay hidden beneath yet more dusty tomes, so that Jennings actually had a place to sit down.

Many of the books had slowly yellowing and faded post-it-notes inside them, Jennings saw, indicating places the Professor had obviously marked out of interest to read later, but though the Detective tried hard to read some of the titles, many of the books appeared to be written in some kind of foreign language that Jennings himself wasn't able to recognise.

"Ahem," the Professor said, coughing loudly, noting the Detectives attention had temporarily wandered away from him. "I take it you *did* actually have a

reason for wanting to come all the way down here and speak to me today, no? I mean, I don't wish to hurry you or anything, but time is money after all and even as we speak, I do still have a *few* important papers that I need to grade for the last few students that I have left. Not to mention several *very* important research papers I need to finish that I *really* ought to be getting on with."
"Sorry, yes, I just got a little bit distracted there for a second,' Detective Jennings said, drawing his attention away from the books on the floor and back to the man he had come all this way down here to meet. "Actually, I was kind of hoping I might talk to you about Bigfoot."
"Ah hah," Professor Clarke said thoughtfully and then sitting back in his chair, somehow found room to rest his feet up on his busy, crowded desk amongst all the books stacked there, as he once more began puffing on his pipe.
"The American Sasquatch, otherwise known as Bigfoot; first properly brought to the public's attention by the now notorious film footage shot by Patterson and Gimlin, way back in the late Nineteen-sixties."
"But that film was just a fake though, right?" Jennings asked. "Just a man in a costume, the last thing I heard."
"That's just what they *want* you to think," the professor said. "There are just as many who claim the footage was an elaborate hoax that swear that on his deathbed, Patterson retracted any previous confessions that he had faked the whole thing, and that he was paid very well while he was alive to keep his silence. Gimlin, himself, has always maintained the footage was real – and at great cost to himself to the point that nowadays, he has all but retreated from the public eye because of all the ridicule he and his family have had to endure these past forty years.
"But I'm pretty sure you didn't come all the way down here to this dusty old basement of mine to ask me my views about a piece of old, antiquated video footage did you? So why don't you tell me what it is you *really* want to know?"
"Well actually," Jennings confessed. " I was kind of wondering if you might know anything at all about a local version of the legend. That is…if you might possibly have heard of something sometimes referred to as 'The Wild-man of Watton','The beast of the A1075', or more often as 'The Thetford Forest Bigfoot'?"
"Why, but of course I have," Professor Hilary Clarke said, suddenly pulling his feet back off the table and puffing out his chest as he sat forward, his interest now all of a sudden piqued by this curious young man sitting here in front of him. He stared at Jennings intently as he attempted to relight his pipe.
"What sort of a hack Cryptozoologist do you take me for?
"Over the past few years, 'The beast of the A1075' has become something of a local legend, almost as famous in Cryptozoology circles as 'the beast of Bodmin

Moor' or 'Black Shuck' himself. But, I'm afraid, if you've come here looking for answers then unfortunately, I'm afraid there's not really that much I can tell you for sadly, unlike its American counterpart, any hard evidence for the existence of such a creature is unfortunately in very short supply."
"Does that mean you don't believe any of the stories are true?" Jennings asked.
"About some sort of primitive creature, some kind of genetic throw-back, living largely undetected, deep in the heart of Thetford forest?' the professor asked, sitting back in his chair and puffing on his pipe once more now he'd finally managed to get it back alight. "I didn't say that,' he said.
"Tell me, have you ever heard of the Coelacanth?"
Jennings shook his head.
"The Coelacanth," the professor explained, "is part of a rare species of fish that was once believed to have become extinct around the time of the Cretaceous period, around 66 million years ago, right up until late December 1938, when a museum curator named Majorie Courtenay-Latimer discovered a living example caught up in the catch of a local angler off the South African coast.
"For a long time, the Coelacanth was thought to be a 'living fossil' – the sole remaining member of a species known only from fossil records – but since then, many more types of Coelacanth have long since been discovered.
"Of course nowadays, the Coelacanth is once again an endangered species and in danger of being made extinct all over again, but that's by the by.
"The Coelacanth is a prime example of something we, in the cryptozoology field, call a 'relict' – a creature that has survived from an earlier period in history and that is one of a few rare examples of a species that is otherwise extinct. Exactly what many of us in the field believe Bigfoot will eventually turn out to be, should a living example ever be discovered.
"And therein lies my problem…
"Tell me, how much do you know about the history of Thetford Forest?"
"Not much," Jennings reluctantly admitted. "I mean, I know the forest isn't a naturally occurring one, and that it was created after The First World War to help replace dwindling timber stocks after the end of the war, but that's about it."
"Well that's more than most," the professor told him, evidently pleased that Jennings had at least done his research. "You're right, of course. After the end of The First World War, the economic future of England looked bleak. Farms were left untenanted and derelict, and large areas of land had been left abandoned especially in areas like Breckland. What would later go on to become The Forestry commission bought up much of the land, and began planting Scots and Corsican pine, along with Douglas Fir and Larch trees - both because of the speed at which they knew they would grow, but also because

those particular trees showed a greater resistance to fungal diseases and insects, exhibited a better tolerance to the thin, chalky soil native to the area, and because they knew the trees would produce a much higher volume of timber per square acre.

"Of course in the years since, the forest has continued to grow and grow and by now far exceeds the size it was back in those days, but here's the thing.

"The only reported sightings of something living in the forest all stem from the last twenty years or so - are all relatively recent – and heavily suggest that whatever it is that might be living out there isn't native to the area, so that begs the question.

"*If there is something living out there, then where did it originally come from?*

"You know, there's nothing I'd like more than the stories people say about something living out there in the woods to be proven true. Can you even begin to comprehend what the discovery of such a creature might do for my career? There's nothing I'd love more. It's the kind of discovery reputations are built on. Unfortunately, the only evidence to suggest such a creature might actually exist all seems to be based solely on conjecture, along with largely uncorroborated and all too often unreliable eye witness accounts.

"To answer your question earlier, do I believe it's possible there might be something living out there in Thetford forest? Yes. Yes I do.

"But do I think it probable? Unfortunately, not so much.

"What I will tell you is this, if there *is* something living out there, then there's probably a very good reason why no-one has been able to find it up until now."

"And what's that?" Jennings asked.

The professor looked at him over his glasses.

"It's because whatever it is that's out there, doesn't want to be found…"

Five

During the night, it snowed.

Not heavily, but enough so that by the time Jennings left his tent the next morning, any tracks that might have been left by the creature or creatures that had visited him during the night were now long gone.

Obliterated and hidden under a thin veil of snow.

Jennings had kept a vigil all night, one hand on his rifle at all times, but the creature, whatever it had been – *Bigfoot,* his mind still insisted – had somewhat disappointingly failed to return. Only somewhat, because after what he had experienced the first time, a small part of Jennings had been only too glad not to have to repeat the same experience again.

Reviewing the footage he had shot the next morning, Jennings was more disappointed to note the evidence on his video camera was hardly the evidence he had been hoping for. For though it was obvious from the video *something* had been out here last night, the night vision footage he had shot was not quite clear enough to be considered conclusive in any way, shape or form.
Jennings had already made up his mind last night to keep on going, but now at least he had one more reason to – for without any decent footage of what he had seen and experienced for himself last night, Jennings knew he would only end up going back to being a laughing stock again if he returned back from leave empty-handed.
And Jennings knew exactly what it was he had seen last night...
Bigfoot.
All he had to do now was prove it.
Packing up his tent and stowing his gear, Jennings arranged himself a small fire and cooked himself up a breakfast of sausage, bacon and eggs as he planned out the next stage of his trip.
Not far away, he knew, only a few miles North, was the River Little Ouse.
A lot further down its banks, several miles and about half a days walk away, the remains of a shredded tent and a couple of sleeping bags had been discovered by the original search party searching for Frank and Amy Hayden, and though there had been little evidence to suggest the abandoned camping gear had definitely been theirs, it had allegedly matched the description of the equipment they were supposed to have brought with them – thus strongly indicating it might just be one of the places where the couple could possibly have set up camp.
Why they might have just have upped and abandoned their camp, and fled leaving their belongings behind them though, was a mystery and one for which the searchers had no answers for.
That wasn't where Jennings was intending to head for though.
He had studied the reports of the search, and spoken to several of the officers and forest rangers who had come out here looking for the missing couple, and had a much different destination in mind.
One of the searchers who had been out here had told him in confidence about an area of the forest where the dogs had steadfastly refused to search. As the searchers had drawn close to the area, the dogs had increasingly become restless and uncooperative – which was most unlike them, and went against all of their training.
The officer in question had described his own feelings as he and the rest of the search party he was with, minus the dog-handlers who had stayed up top with their dogs, had descended down to the small stream that the dogs had refused to

approach and had told Jennings he too had felt more than a little uncomfortable heading down there.

"We didn't find anything, nor see anything down there neither," the officer had told him, "but all the while, all of us had the strangest feeling like we were being watched. Gave us all the heebie-jeebies, so it did, and yet none of us who went down there could quite put our finger on why that should be the case."

The officer he was speaking to had been one of those who had given Jennings so much shit all those years ago, back when Chris had had his own experience out here in the woods – during his investigation into one of the very first official reported sightings of the 'Thetford Forest Bigfoot'- but if the officer in question remembered that now, the irony appeared lost on him.

Chris hadn't though.

He still remembered it like it was yesterday.

Not so smug now, are you? Jennings remembered thinking at the time, but instead of saying that out loud, he had settled instead for asking what the officer's superiors had said when he had told *them* about the incident down by the brook and the strange behaviour of the search and rescue dogs.

"Didn't want to know, did they?" The officer had said. "Told me it was probably nothing, that the dogs probably just got a scent of another animal – a deer or something – or probably just smelled something they didn't like, and that the main focus of the search was to prioritise where the shredded tent and abandoned camping equipment was found. Thing is though, I spoke to one of the dog handlers later when we were grabbing a pint down the local pub after we'd finished for the day, and *he* told me he'd never seen his dogs react that way before in thirty years of being a dog handler. I mean, he said he'd seen them get spooked before, but never anything quite like that…"

Jennings had got the officer to provide him with the co-ordinates of the exact location where the dogs had gotten spooked, and convinced him to point the spot out on a map of the forest, and that was where he was intending to head out towards today.

It would probably turn out to be nothing and a total waste of his time, Jennings thought, but it was less than half a days walk from where he was now and if it *did* all turn out to be nothing but a wild goose chase, it should still leave him plenty enough time before nightfall to head back over to where the abandoned tent had been found and set up camp for the night there.

In one of the last places it was thought Frank and Amy Hayden might have been, shortly before their return to their car and their subsequent disappearance.

Nothing ventured, nothing gained, Jennings thought, and stamping out his fire, started to pack up his camp.

***

As Jennings started walking through the forest, a few minutes later, he dug out his video camera and began speaking into it once more – recording an update on his progress so far following the events of the previous night.

The footage from last night was on a separate memory card, currently being stored in his backpack, and Jennings planned to edit everything together at a much later date when he was back home and safely out of this forest.

"Day Two," Jennings said into the camera, "and after the visit to my camp last night by creature or creatures unknown, I am continuing my journey deep into the heart of Thetford Forest in search of what might have happened to missing campers, Frank and Amy Hayden. My destination this morning, to an area of the forest several miles away where it has been reliably reported to me that search and rescue dogs exhibited uncharacteristic behaviour during the recent search for the missing campers, shortly before they were called away to another site following the discovery of an abandoned tent that may or may not have belonged to the Haydens.

"I'll be checking out that site at a later date, maybe this afternoon if I make good timing, but for now, at least, I want to try and discover what might have disturbed the search and rescue dogs so. Could be nothing, could be something, but a feeling in my gut tells me it's worth checking out anyway – even if it does prove to be a total and complete waste of time."

Jennings stopped recording, switched off the video camera, and then paused while he stowed it back in his backpack.

Still wearing his ghillie suit so he blended in with his surroundings, Jennings unshouldered his rifle and took one last look all around him.

Though he couldn't actually *see* anything, Jennings still couldn't seem to shake the feeling that he was being watched, and wanted to be ready just in case whatever it was that had visited him last night had decided to come back.

But there was nothing.

The forest was silent.

Not so much as the sound of anything moving or even a single bird singing in the trees.

Taking a second to consult his map, Jennings took a compass reading, and then started heading off in the direction he thought he needed to be going.

Behind him, in the forest, unseen, whatever it was that had been watching him the day before, slowly began to follow him once more…

Six

Jennings had been walking through the forest for about three hours when he first started to suspect he might be lost.
By now, he thought, he must surely be drawing close to the area his colleague had described - the creek where it was said the dogs on the previous search were supposed to have become so unsettled - but so far Jennings had seen no sign of any of the landmarks his colleague had described, and was now slowly starting to suspect that somehow he must have taken a wrong turn somewhere.
And though he had tried a couple of times to take a map reading, to try and ascertain exactly where he was, even his compass so far seemed to be proving useless. On the one time he had tried to consult it to make sure he was still on track and headed in the right direction, the needle had continued to spin round constantly and had steadfastly refused to settle on North.
It suggested some kind of massive magnetic disturbance, but the only place he had ever heard of that happening locally before was over in neighbouring Rendlesham Forest – well known for its UFO sightings, and supposedly the site of a flying saucer crash way back in the eighties.
Jennings did not believe in UFOs and aliens - Bigfoot was one thing, that was perfectly feasible, but aliens…nah, that was a step too far – but he had been out in Rendlesham Forest, and seen for himself first-hand the way electrical equipment often malfunctioned for no apparent reason, and the way compasses would often refuse to function, a bit like now.
For fuck's sake, Jennings thought. *It's just a cheap, dodgy compass.*
But he couldn't help the way it was making him feel on edge, not knowing exactly where he was going. Jennings was a bit of a control freak - always had been, always would be – and so knowing he wasn't currently in full control of his situation certainly wasn't helping the anxiety he was feeling because of all that had happened the night before.
Just need to keep going and hope for the best, Jennings thought.
But though he couldn't see anything, still he couldn't seem to shake the feeling of being watched…

***

"I saw something out there once. Not Bigfoot itself, but…something…."
Back in the Professor's basement, deep beneath the university, Jennings was recounting his own experiences out there in the woods that day, all those years ago, back when his curiosity – some might say obsession - with Thetford Forest, and whatever it was that might be out there, had first been awoken.
Professor Hilary Clarke listened to what Jennings had to say, then sat back puffing heavily on his pipe.

"And you say you never actually saw the creature itself?" The Professor asked when the young man sat in front of him was finally done with his tale.
"Well…no…" Jennings said, "but…"
"But you never saw the creature itself – whatever it was the family claimed to have seen and indeed, would have you believe they struck back there on the road that night, out on the A1075?"
"Well, no," Jennings reluctantly confessed.
"So what makes *you* think there's really anything out there?"
"I don't know," Jennings admitted. "I guess it was just a gut feeling – that something was out there, I mean. That grisly tableau I stumbled across? That was gone by the time the other officers arrived? That couldn't have been the work of just kids. Kids would have just left it there. They wouldn't have come back and tidied some of it back up before I arrived back on the scene just to fuck with me.
"Too much effort.
"No, there was definitely something out there that day, I'm sure of it."
"You should always listen to your gut," the professor said. "It's racial memory – part of your survival instinct, passed down generation after generation by your ancestors, going back to when we are lived in caves. Most phobias and modern day fears stem from our racial memory, going back tens of hundreds of years, and are what kept us alive all those many thousands of years ago.
"And they all manifest themselves in the same way – through our gut.
"Gut instinct - there's a lot to be said for it, and yet so many of us nowadays are so quick to dismiss it."
"Tell me something," Jennings asked, slightly changing the subject. "You said earlier that you believe it's possible there's something out there – in Thetford Forest, I mean – so I guess what I'm asking…well, why haven't you ever gone hunting for it?"
The professor stared at him for a moment before answering.
"Because it's a young man's game," he eventually replied. "I'm a scholar, always have been, not an adventurer. Research is *my* game, not hunting down mythical monsters. Besides, I'm hardly what you'd call an 'outdoorsy' type.
"I was ever really built for camping out and sleeping under the stars."
He indicated the basement all around him.
"This is as far as I have ever wanted to travel."
"You're scared," Jennings said, suddenly realising the truth. "You think there *is* something out there, but you're too afraid to go out there and find out for yourself."
"And can you blame me?" The professor asked him, looking Jennings straight in the eye. "A lot of people have disappeared out there, over the years. A hell of

a lot more than the authorities are willing to admit. And you know what they say…"
"No," Jennings said. "What do they say?"
"Two things," the professor told him. "They say two things – one, curiosity killed the cat, and two, sometimes it's best just to let sleeping dogs lie.
"If you really *are* thinking of going out there, just take one little piece of advice with you – make sure you're the hunter, not the hunted…"

***

Walking through the forest now, the professor's words suddenly came back to him, and Jennings had to fight hard to suppress a shiver down his spine.
All of a sudden, those words – words he had so easily dismissed back then – were suddenly starting to feel a hell of a lot more relevant.
He was doing all this for the right reasons, he told himself. Trying to earn some kind of closure for Frank and Amy Hayden's family, but was that all there was to it?
After the incident last night, Jennings was slowly starting to question just what he really was out here the further that he walked – hunted, or hunter?
If you'd have asked him the same question twenty-fours ago, Jennings thought, he probably would have given you a different answer, but now? After last night? Suddenly, in the cold light of a brand new day, Jennings was starting to think he wasn't quite so sure anymore.
It didn't help that out here, in the quiet forest, all that he had was time to think. His brain was constantly churning, ticking over; it was like he just couldn't switch off. If there had been something else out here, some kind of wildlife or any sign of animals, even some birdsong, then it might have helped distract him as he walked.
But out here, in the middle of the forest, there was nothing.
Just him out here, alone with his thoughts.
Jennings almost thought he could kind of understand now how people lost in the wilderness, in total isolation, could often go crazy when left alone with just their thoughts for company.
Cabin fever, wasn't that what they called it?
Jennings had only been out here for just over a day, but already he felt as though his experiences of the previous night were starting to make him feel paranoid – even as camouflaged and disguised as he was.
It was only as he came out of a clearing in the woods, that Jennings suddenly realised where he was.
Somehow, he thought, he must have gotten all turned around and headed off in completely the opposite, and wrong, direction to where he had wanted to be

going, for Jennings had just emerged, and now found himself, at the ruined campsite searchers had discovered when originally looking for the missing campers, Frank and Amy Hayden.

Any evidence that had been here at the time had all been taken away and sent to the labs for testing, but Jennings had seen the photos and so was still fairly confident that this was exactly where the shredded tent and sleeping bags had been found.

He remembered reading the lab reports – illicitly of course, because officially he was not supposed to be looking into the case – and apparently the results had come back inconclusive. The tent, and the sleeping bags, had both been saturated at some point in animal urine – a bit like how certain animals and mammals marked their territory – but as to when it might possibly have happened, the lab had been unable to say.

They had also been unable to confirm or deny the animal(s?) that may have been responsible, but had only been able to say for certain that the urine sample they had tested was definitely not human.

Of course, this only left a wide variety of other choices.

Unfortunately, they had been unable to test if the urine had come from a Sasquatch because, presently, no such comparison test existed, but after last night, Jennings was pretty sure he knew exactly what the results would have been had the test been available.

Grade A positive all the fucking way...

Looking around, Jennings decided to set up camp for the night here.

He had obviously been in the forest walking for much longer than he'd realised, he thought, because already the sun was just beginning to set.

Hell, he only thought he'd been walking a few hours, but somehow he had managed to skip lunch and walk long into the afternoon.

Jennings raised his wrist and looked down at his watch.

Like his compass much earlier, the hands on his watch were acting all screwy – travelling round the wrong way, anti-clockwise, and at a much faster pace than they were supposed to. Both the minute and the hour hand were now moving round at the same speed as the second hand which, curiously by the way, was still moving in the correct direction he noted.

Cheap piece of shit, he thought, in an echo of what he had said earlier about the compass. But it had been a present from his mum, twenty years ago, just before she'd finally succumbed to cancer, so for obvious reasons he was reluctant to remove it.

Looking up, Jennings saw the sky was a furious blood red.

It almost looked like the sun was bleeding into the sky, or on fire or something, and again he found himself wondering how it could suddenly be so late.

It could be only one of three things, he decided. Either he had been the victim of missing time, like people often described when they claimed to have been abducted by aliens; or time was running differently here, just like Jennings had heard people say sometimes happened in Rendlesham Forest; or he had obviously fallen into some kind of fugue state, some kind of trance while he was walking and so had just lost all sense or track of time.
Neither of which option particularly reassured him that something weird hadn't been going on out here from the moment he came out here.
Finished setting up his camp for the night, Jennings thought about that old saying the local farmers always said around here.
Red sky at night, shepherds delight. Red sky in the morning, shepherds warning.
Right now, Jennings could think of nothing delightful about the bright red sunset he was seeing.
In fact, it almost felt like something ominous…
He unshouldered his rifle, made himself something to eat – surprisingly not that hungry for someone who supposedly had been walking all day, even though he could remember very little of it - and setting up his camera again as he had last night, settled down to wait out the night.
This time if anything came for him, Jennings intended to be ready…

Seven

Jennings caught a couple of hours sleep before he was disturbed again. Sitting by his camera, set up at the entrance to his tent – his rifle close to hand this time – he must have drifted off, he reckoned, because the next thing Jennings knew he was being startled awake by noises and sounds coming from the forest all around him.
There were strange howls, the sound of something crying out into the night, and the sound of several others answering whatever it was that was making the call. He could hear branches cracking, and the sound of something – or several somethings – moving heavily about in the trees beyond his little campsite, but when he looked through his camera, pointed at the tree line, he could see nothing, even with the night vision on.
Somehow that made it worse.
He kept scanning the tree-line, trying to minimise his movement in case there really *was* anything out there, but if there was he just couldn't see it.
He tried to tell himself the cracking of branches and the sounds he was hearing were just the natural sounds of the forest, and the howls he could hear just foxes

mating – when they really got into it, the sound of two foxes going 'at it' could sound like human screams, and he had answered many an emergency call in the past that had turned out to be nothing more than a pair of foxes enjoying themselves – but it was the wrong season for that, and mating would not begin again for another couple of months.
And besides, whatever was out there was too big to be foxes.
Something brushed by his tent, something big and heavy, and as brave as he was Jennings still had to bite back a scream.
A big black shadow passed across the canvas, followed by another going in the opposite direction.
A loud, bellowing roar split the air, followed by another just outside his tent. Jennings froze in fear, just as he had the night before.
Whatever had visited his campsite last night was back again, there was more than one, and they were right outside.
He didn't think they would be able to see his tent, for he had disguised it again with leaves and branches just as he had the night before, but they had probably found the remains of the campfire he had cooked his good on before retiring, and no doubt could probably smell him; smell his fear.
It was a well known fact that fear produced certain chemicals and pheromones in the body that some animals could detect, and Jennings just hoped and prayed that wasn't true about Sasquatch.
There was a grunt from just by the entrance to his tent, and the sound of something large sniffing the air – like a dog, or a wolf, he thought – and then another loud roar.
Jennings was so afraid of alerting whatever was out there to his presence, he could not even look through the viewfinder of his camera. The slightest movement, he knew, might give his position away at any moment and the video camera was definitely still recording – he could hear the little whir of the machine going round – so at the very least, whatever was out there at least he was getting it on film.
More roars sounded, and more howls.
Christ, you've made your fucking point – why don't you just fuck off already for Christ's sake, Jennings thought, but the sounds of something or somethings moving around out there continued to echo through the forest. *How many of the fecking things* are *there out there?* He wondered.
There was the sound of something splattering against the wall of the tent and for a second, Jennings thought it must have started raining.
But then he realised the truth – whatever was out there was pissing on him…urinating on the side of his tent.

Thankfully the tent was waterproof so it wouldn't soak through, but that didn't take away from the fact that *something* was still pissing on his tent.
And it stank.
It absolutely stank.
A stench of ammonia, mixed with something else he couldn't immediately identify, filled the tent, making him want to gag, and retch - except he couldn't, not without giving himself away. Instead he had to bite back his rising bile, and try to swallow it, which almost made him bring it all back up again.
He thought back to the lab reports he had read of the abandoned and shredded tent and camping gear they had found out here – of how they had found traces of some kind of animal urine soaked into the canvass – and instantly knew what the creature out there was doing.
It was establishing its dominance over another animal that had entered its hunting grounds; was marking its territory. Warning other animals, other hunters to stay away. Or, if it knew he was here, hiding, maybe it was even trying to intimidate him a little bit.
But that was suggesting the creature out there was capable of far more than just the crude intellect that studies into Sasquatch Jennings had previously read would suggest, and that in actual fact whatever was out there was in possession of some kind of rudimentary intelligence.
Did that mean he might be able to communicate with the creature? Jennings thought. Reason with it even?
Another mighty roar that once more split the night indicated otherwise.
Whatever it was that was out there finished pissing on his tent and started to move away, and Jennings breathed out a sigh of relief he hadn't realised he was holding.
If he thought he might have pissed himself a little last night, he thought, then he definitely had tonight – no question.
Fuck! He thought. *The creature had been right there, practically in top of him. And it was only luck,* he strongly suspected, *and the crude camouflage he had used to disguise his tent that had probably prevented the same thing happening to him as had presumably happened to Frank and Amy Hayden while they were out here.*
If they had only experienced a third of what he had had to endure the past couple of nights, then was it any wonder they had tried to flee leaving much of their stuff behind.
Fuck! He thought. *Fuck, fuck, fuck. For a minute there, he had been convinced he was going to die.*
There was a roar from just outside the back of his tent, and Jennings felt his bladder let go once more.

Shit, it was still out there, he thought. *Still right outside his fecking tent!!!*
It was playing with him, Jennings thought. *Taunting him; waiting for him to make a move and reveal himself...and he very nearly had!*
Jennings froze where he was, not daring even so much as to breathe as he decided to play the creature at its own game.
Come on then, he thought. *Come on then you motherfucker.*
He had been on stakeouts that had lasted for days at a time.
Had meant sleeping in his car and barely moving other than to go to the toilet when it was absolutely necessary – and even then, pissing into a bottle – or grabbing a quick bite to eat to keep his strength and his wits up.
Oh, such stakeouts were rare now in modern policing – but he had done it numerous times when they hadn't even been supposed to have been watching their prey, and hadn't been issued an official court order to say they could observe the perp, and so this, to him, was nothing.
He could wait here all night if he had to.
Two could play that game, he thought.
If he had been more sure how many others were out there, Jennings might have risked it, bundled out of the tent and tried shooting the creature standing over him with his rifle – but he *didn't* know how many more of the creatures was out here with him tonight, or exactly what he was dealing with.
If he *did* hit the creature out there, and only wounded it and didn't kill it, he might just end up making it mad and the last thing Jennings thought he wanted was an angry Sasquatch in his face.
It was bad enough the creature was even out there in the first place.
As he sat there, frozen in place, unable to move so much as an inch in case his movement gave him away, Jennings heard the creatures breathing patterns starting to change. It's breathing became much more slower, and deeper, and then there was a sound that at first, Jennings didn't recognise.
And then he realised what it was.
Was that...was that snoring? He thought. It sounded like the Bigfoot, the Sasquatch, whatever it was out there must have fallen asleep!
Finally able to move, but still keeping his movements to a minimum, Jennings stretched out and relaxed his grip on his rifle a little bit.
At some point, he feel asleep as well.
And when he woke back up again several hours later, the creatures were gone.

Eight

"Stick to the waterways."
"I'm sorry?"
"If you're really serious about trying to track down this thing, then stick to the River Little Ouse; all the little streams and the brooks that run all the way through Thetford Forest. All the latest studies, the most up-to-date research, they all suggest Sasquatch, if they do in fact exist, are most likely to be found by bodies of water. They follow the waterways, you see. That's how they move about. Nearly all of the sightings that occurred these past few years? They've all occurred near or close by to rivers or streams."
Detective Inspector Chris Jennings was still down in the professor's basement. He had been down here now for nearly two hours, talking to the professor, and by now his throat was starting to get a bit dry, breathing in all the stale, dusty air down here in this dark, windowless room.
Thankfully the professor had long since put out his pipe, but with nowhere for the smoke to really go, the cloying, heady smell of pipe tobacco still hung in the air, slowly filling his lungs and throat.
"Don't get me wrong – I still think you're a fool for trying to track down whatever's out there, but if you're going to go looking, you might as well look in the right place."

***

Now, as he walked along the bank, following the course of the river, Jennings thought back to everything the old man had said.
Everything the ageing professor had told him.
Today Jennings' compass appeared to be working fine; his watch, too – both working perfectly normal again, as though nothing had ever been wrong with them yesterday.
As he followed the coordinates his colleague had given him to the site he had been intending to visit yesterday, where the Search and Rescue dogs had allegedly began acting strange, Jennings idly wondered if something in the forest might have been affecting him yesterday – explaining away the enormous sense of displacement he had felt all day yesterday, along with the missing time he thought he might have experienced.
Some kind of hallucinogen or something.
Maybe there was some kind of plant, or fungus, out here and he had breathed in their pollen or spores and that was what had affected him, and there had never been anything wrong with his compass or watch, he thought.

It made as much sense as anything else – but it still did not explain away his little visit last night from creature, or creatures, unknown.
Bigfoot, his mind still insisted.
But Jennings was a realist, a pragmatist, and still wasn't quite prepared to accept that fully without some kind of hard evidence to back it up.
Oh, he believed it was highly probable something was living out here in these woods – and had done for the past twenty years since his last experience out here – and he still believed it was very likely some kind of Sasquatch had visited him in the night, but as a police officer, evidence was everything and since he still hadn't got any concrete and conclusive footage yet, that still left room for plenty of other possibilities.
Including someone trying to fuck with him.
Plenty of his colleagues had known he was coming out here this weekend, and what he was hoping to prove, and he wouldn't put it past any of them to decide to pull a prank on him and mess with his head while he was out here.
But even that still didn't completely explain what he had woken up to this morning – a scene like something you might expect to find in an abattoir; either that or an eighties splatterpunk movie.
Bloody guts and entrails from numerous animals had been littered all across the place where he had made camp last night and right by the entrance to his tent, a stag's head had been jammed on top of a sharpened wooden stake and left there for him to find, in a grisly echo of the same scene he had stumbled across when he had been investigating his first Bigfoot sighting over twenty years ago now.
Both of the creatures eyes had been put out, and there seemed to be an almost ritualistic theme to the way the bloody guts and entrails had all been strung about the campsite - not to mention the way the staked head had almost been left for him like some kind of a warning.
Or maybe that was just his brain's way of trying to make some sort of sense out of the sheer randomness of it all, he thought.
Some of the entrails and intestines had been hung from nearby trees, and the whole area all around him quite literally looked like a bloodbath.
Along with the stench of Sasquatch piss from his tent, where his visitor - or visitors - last night had decided to mark their territory, there had also been a coppery scent to the air that reminded Jennings of some of the worst crime scenes he'd ever visited during his long time spent on the job.
Like the kid who had attempted to remove all of his skin, before trying to do the same to both his mother and step-father.
Or the father who had taken a sledgehammer to his wife and twin girls, and smashed in their skulls like he was breaking into an egg.

The scene he had woken up to this morning was nowhere near as bad as either of those, but still it had come pretty close.
It looked like whatever animals the guts and entrails might have belonged to, their bodies had quite literally been torn apart.
Jennings had checked his camera from the night before, but it had obviously fallen over at some stage in the night because all you could see on the viewfinder during playback was a close-up of the sides of the tent.
You could clearly hear the roars coming from somewhere outside, along with the sound of something big, something massive moving past the tent; and then a few minutes later, the splatter of it's piss on the canvas of the tent; followed a series of loud ripping sounds which had obviously been the noise of whatever animal or animals the visiting Bigfoot had decided to tear apart.
But that was it.
Added to the footage of the previous night, it still amounted to not very much at all – hell, that Blair Witch film from a few years back had offered more convincing evidence of something weird happening out in the woods, and that was made up and had been filmed on a shoestring budget.
After everything that happened the last two nights, everything inside of Jennings was quite literally screaming at him to just pack up and go home; was telling him that after last night, he was putting his life in danger by staying out here. But after what had happened yesterday with the compass and the missing time, he thought, there was no guarantee he would even be able to find his way back to the car, let alone be allowed to drive out of the forest even should he attempt to do so.
Frank and Amy Hayden had obviously tried that, and look what had happened to them.
Except that was the whole point wasn't it?
No-one knew what had happened to them.
And that was the whole reason he was out here in the first place.
He had made a vow to discover the truth, and the one thing Jennings always did was keep his promises – even those he had only made to himself.
Jennings had had a wash in the river, washed all his clothes, and tried to get the smell of Sasquatch piss out of his tent in vain, before eating a light breakfast, packing up, and setting off once again.
Determined, today, to reach where he'd been trying to head to yesterday.
All that had been nearly three hours ago now…

***

Now, Jennings was still walking, with no sign yet of the location he was supposed to be headed for. Part of him wondered if he might possibly be lost again and feeling paranoid, kept checking his watch and compass to make sure a) he was still headed in the right direction, and b) that he wasn't experiencing any more mysterious lapses in time.

But today, everything was normal.

Normal except for the silence of the forest.

For just as yesterday, there was not a sound to be heard – not even the sound of birdsong. It was unnaturally quiet, Jennings thought, and that only added to the anxiety he was already feeling.

As he walked, the big question Jennings kept asking himself was, was he doing the right thing by continuing on? He couldn't shake the feeling that his visits the past couple of nights, coupled with the grisly scene left for him this morning, had both been meant as a warning and that by continuing on, he was only being foolhardy.

But again, he told himself, he had made a vow to discover the truth about Frank and Amy Hayden's disappearance, and he refused to be scared off by what essentially, was no more than a dumb beast.

A deadly beast, true – and one much more deadly than he'd originally thought, especially if he was right in what he suspected and there really was more than one Bigfoot out here – but a dumb beast nonetheless.

That didn't mean he should underestimate the creature, or creatures, by any means, he thought. But it did mean by rights, he *should* be able to outthink them. He just had to try and second guess them was all.

Frank and Amy Hayden, wherever they might be now, hadn't known what they were dealing with out here.

He did.

And that, *that* was the difference...

***

Jennings finally reached his destination sometime around noon.

By the time he arrived, he was fairly certain he must have walked around in a circle a few times, as he was positive he had already passed through the exact same part of the forest at least twice, but he had no way of telling for sure and was just happy he had eventually come out where he wanted.

Jennings checked the coordinates of his location with those he had been given by his colleague, and was suitably confident he had arrived at the right place. Sitting back by the bank of a small stream to grab a quick lunch of dried meat and fruit – goji berries to give him energy – Jennings looked around himself and took in his surroundings.

He appeared to be in some kind of bluff, or gully – the tall, steep banks rising up out of sight on either side of him.

A gentle brook, or stream, ran along the entire length of the bluff for several miles, as far as the eye could see, disappearing off into the trees.

If he wasn't precisely where the Search and Rescue dogs had started to get antsy, he thought, then he couldn't be far off, and resolved to follow the stream for as far as it ran.

He was wearing the ghillie suit again, just as he had the past couple of days, after washing it in the river early this morning so it didn't smell of his sweat. Now, he reached down into the small river and rubbed wet mud on his face and cheeks.

He had no idea how the Bigfoot, or Sasquatch if that's what they were, had known exactly where he was last night, for once more he had disguised his tent so it was camouflaged and blended in with his surroundings, but he thought they must be tracking him.

If so, he didn't intend to make things easy for them.

Satisfied that *he* was now able to blend in with his environment, Jennings set off down the stream; moving slowly and steadily to try and minimise any noise he might make.

He had been travelling for about a mile when he saw it, and if he hadn't been paying attention, he quite easily could have missed it.

The entrance to a massive hole in the ground, almost hidden by the roots of a fallen tree that stretched out over it, practically concealing it from the naked eye. He didn't know what about it had caught his eye, and if he had been looking anywhere else, he surely would have passed it without even realising it was there, but he wasn't and so, as he walked along the bank of the stream, Jennings made the decision to go and check it out and investigate.

As he approached, Jennings looked all around him for any signs of habitation anywhere nearby – animal droppings, or faeces, or anything – just in case there was any evidence the hole was a den for some kind of animal - but there was nothing.

Ducking under the roots of the fallen tree, Jennings approached the entrance. It was a lot bigger than he'd thought when he'd first noticed it and for a moment, he wondered how anyone searching out here could possibly have missed seeing it – but then, he thought, if it hadn't been for chance; a remote stroke of luck; fate, kismet, karma…whatever, he too might just as easily have passed it by none-the-wiser.

There was an almost animal-like smell coming out of the den – for that, he supposed, was precisely what it was; some animal's den; what else could it possibly be? – that reminded him of trips to the zoo when he was a little boy, mixed with the smell of dirt.

It almost kind of smelled like wet, shaggy dog after rain on a traditional British summer's afternoon, but there was something else there too - something he could not, as yet, define.
Jennings pulled out a torch and shone it down into the hole to try and see just how far it stretched, but there was no way of telling. The black tunnel turned a corner and just seemed to keep on going.
It was almost tall enough for him to stand upright in.
Almost…but not quite.
Jennings stood there for a moment, not quite sure what he should do, and then, finally, he made a decision.
He needed to find out how far down it went, he realised.
He needed to go in…

Nine

Jennings stood at the entrance to the hole.
There had been rumours of an underground cave system and a series of tunnels beneath Thetford Forest ever since the Forestry Commission had built an artificial hibernaculum a few years back - not only to give some of the local fauna a place of shelter during the cold winter months, but also as part of an educational programme that the Commission promoted with local schools and youth centres.
Thetford Forest was home to over a dozen varying and different species of bats, many of them rare, and as an endangered species, the hibernaculum – a purposely built underground cave system – was the Forestry Commissions way of trying to preserve the animals and keep them safe in as close to a natural environment that they could create.
During construction of the cave, a series of interlocking underground tunnels and caverns had been discovered, but had remained largely undisturbed and unexplored after being deemed unsafe and liable to collapse should they investigate any further.
Entrance to those underground caverns had been blocked up - and the Forestry Commission had downplayed the whole thing and made out the tunnels were not of any significant scientific interest - and so there was no way of possibly knowing how far they might reach. Their very presence had been all but ignored by the mainstream media and local press, and it was only because of his extensive research that Jennings had even learnt of their existence.

Grimes Graves, the flint mine and popular tourist attraction, was only a few miles away in the other direction, and there was also STANTA, the Stanford Training Area owned by the British Army only a few miles away as well. Access to the military training ground was strictly prohibited to the general public because it was classed as a live firing area, but there had been rumours for years that the army had built a series of fox-holes and bunkers there to simulate the kind of battle soldiers might experience underground over in Iraq and the Middle East whilst hunting Al-Qaeda, and that many of the caverns and tunnels had already been present and the British Army had just extended and expanded on what had already been there.

This massive hole in the ground, Jennings thought, could be something to do with any, either, or all of them. If it connected to the military tunnels, he could be in serious trouble if he got caught down there, Jennings thought, and if it was related to the tunnels the Forestry Commission had discovered whilst building their hide-out for bats, there was the danger of collapse.

Jennings would be at risk of being buried alive.

The best option, out of all of them, was that it was just an animal's den – some kind of warren perhaps – and that he would not be able to travel very far before the roof of the tunnel got smaller and smaller and unable to progress any further, he would be forced to head back the way he had come in.

Worst case scenario – other than being buried alive, or being arrested on charges of spying and espionage and being sent to a remote interrogation centre – was that the hole led down, deep down, into the Sasquatch's lair, and that was why sightings of them over the years had been so rare.

They spent most of their time underground.

But that was just silly, he thought. He had no way of knowing quite what to expect, unless he pulled up his big-boy pants and decided to venture inside.

Nothing ventured, Jennings told himself, *nothing gained.*

He did his best to try and ignore the other two sayings that were going round his head - *Curiosity killed the cat*...and, *come into my parlour said the spider to the fly*...

***

Jennings took out his video camera and setting it up a few feet away from himself, pressed record.

"Day three of my investigation into the missing campers, Frank and Amy Hayden," he began, "and even after last night's violent incursion onto my campsite by creature, or creatures, unknown, I have, perhaps somewhat foolhardily, decided to continue my search. I am standing now at the location where Search and Rescue dogs are reputed to have started acting strangely, shortly before being called away to another site of specific interest, and have discovered a massive hole in the earth, partly concealed under a fallen tree – possibly explaining why searchers neglected to find it during their earlier sweep of this location.

"I have no idea how far this cavern stretches, or how safe it may be inside, so I am making this recording now as an official record of my intentions, just in case anything should befall me while I am down there.

"It is the closest thing to a lead to where the missing campers may have possibly disappeared to that anyone has found so far, so I feel like I need to investigate in my bid to discover the truth.

"I will leave this camera close by the entrance to the cave mouth, just in case if I do not return and anyone comes searching for, me they will find this recording and know where I have gone. This is Detective Inspector Christopher Andrew Jennings temporarily signing off."

He switched off the recording and hung the camera by a branch of a nearby tree, pointing towards the cave mouth. He activated the motion sensor on the camera so that if he, or anything else emerged, there would instantly be a recording of what came back out, should anything happen to him down there.

Part of him was really afraid, terrified in fact, and knew that what he was about to do was really, *really,* stupid, but another part also knew he could not just leave here and return later with reinforcements - both because there was a small chance that whatever was down there in the tunnels might close and seal them off if they thought they had been discovered, and he would be made to look like a laughing stock again; but also because he had a naturally inquisitive instinct and a big part of him actually *wanted* to go down there and see what was what.

Jennings unshouldered his rifle, took off his backpack, and removed anything that was not essential to try and minimise what he would be taking down there. He kept back a torch, more dried fruit and meat, bottles of water and spare ammunition for the rifle, and removed anything else like a spare battery and recording discs for the camera and his map, which he couldn't see him needing while he was down there.

That done, and finally sure he was now only carrying with him anything that was essential or might be useful, Jennings steeled his nerve and prepared himself to enter the cave mouth.

The smell was even worse inside than it had been by the entrance, he thought. It smelled like *something* had been sleeping down here, and Jennings only hoped the family he had interviewed all those years ago on his first trip out here had been wrong and it *wasn't* a bear, or even a family of bears, living out here – though in some ways that at least would have been preferable to a family of Sasquatch, for at least he thought he had some kind of idea what behaviour to expect from a bear.

The Sasquatch though? They were an unknown quantity.
So far, although the Bigfoot – if that *was* what had visited him in the night – appeared to have threatened him, they hadn't yet attacked him or physically caused him harm, and for all he knew, might well be friendly.
Or, much more likely, they might not be.
He remembered the words of the professor he'd visited, down in the university basement, and what the old man had told him – '*if no-one has ever discovered anything living out there until now, maybe there's a reason for that. Maybe whatever's out there doesn't want to be found!*'
Jennings suppressed a shiver, and took his first step down into the massive black hole leading deep underground.
The walls were firm and looked like they had been carved out of the earth – but whether or not the tunnel had been dug out, or whether it was naturally occurring, Jennings really couldn't say.
Geography had never exactly been his strong point.
The cave entrance opened up into a tunnel that led round the next corner and out of sight and so, lighting up his torch, Jennings tentatively started to follow the tunnel down into the inky, black depths.
The further he walked, the less the smell down here appeared to bother him – or maybe he was just becoming acclimatised to it, he thought absentmindedly.
Thick roots dangled and stretched out all along the ceiling – presumably from trees growing overhead – and lined the tunnel walls. Shining his torch in front of him, Jennings attempted to try and make out just how far ahead the tunnel stretched, but could see nothing,
It seemed to go on for miles, and showed no sign of getting smaller – which was good, he thought, for walking hunched over was already making his progress slow, uncomfortable and cumbersome.
Not for a minute did he consider turning round and heading back.
He felt a little like Theseus, walking down into the deep, dark depths of the labyrinth to confront the Minotaur, and wished he had someone like Ariadne waiting for him back up top. At the very least, he thought, he should've brought with him some yarn, some rope, or some string so that he could find his way back to the surface, but it was much too late for all that now.
Back when he had been much younger, one of his favourite shows as a kid had been an adaption of The Adventures of Tom Sawyer and Huckleberry Finn. One of the most terrifying episodes for him as a child had been the one where Tom and Becky wandered off in a cave and got lost. They had been found eventually and been rescued, but that particular episode had given him nightmares for a week back then of being trapped underground, and had stayed with him ever since all the way into adulthood.

Likewise, about a year ago, he had taken a girl out on a date with him to the cinema, and they had watched a little film called The Descent.
This too had involved a group of spelunkers going down into a cave system and becoming trapped, and had again given him nightmares for about a week of being hunted alone in the dark, trapped underground.
And now, here he was doing this – voluntarily travelling underground to explore a cave system he had found because he had promised a vow to a pair of missing campers to find them, or at the very least discover what had happened to them.
He really *must* be stupid, he thought. But then, he only intended go down a little way, just to see how far the tunnel went, and then he would head back, he promised himself.
As soon as it looked like the way ahead looked like it was in danger of collapsing, or started to narrow too much for him to continue, he would turn around and head back out to the surface again, he told himself.
As he slowly descended further and further down the tunnel, Jennings felt the first stirrings of claustrophobia starting to kick in, enclosed as he was by walls of dirt and soil.
He paused to drink from a bottle of water from his pack, then looked back the way he'd come and realised he'd walked further than he'd thought already.
The last glimmer of daylight that held still been able to see, even after turning the corner of the tunnel, was now gone and behind him lay the same thing that awaited him dead ahead – complete and total darkness.
The smell this far down was less animal-like in nature, and more like damp, wet soil after a heavy rainfall. More tree roots lined the roof and walls than before, and Jennings could see insects and bugs crawling amongst them, and falling down onto his shoulders and torso and even, he thought, his head.
He brushed his hand through his hair and tried, and failed, to suppress a shiver.
Just a bit further, he told himself. *A little bit more further and I'll turn around and head back.*
He tried to regulate his breathing, fighting the panic he could feel building in him as the tunnel opened up a bit more, at least allowing him to walk a bit more upright now instead of hunched over.
He turned a corner, tripped on an exposed root, and fell down a bit of a slope.
When he opened his eyes again, he found himself in a huge open cavern.
Thankfully his torch had survived his short fall, and it was only as he shone it along the walls of the room that he now found himself in that he suddenly realised precisely what he had just stumbled into.
He had been right in his earlier estimations, he thought.

This tunnel that he had found obviously *was* used by the Sasquatch and what was more, the cavern he had just fallen into appeared, for all intents and purposes, to be the Bigfoot's lair!

Ten

Jennings stood where he was for a moment, looking around.
The animal smell he had smelled earlier, back at the cave mouth, back the way he'd just come, was stronger here again and much more prevalent.
There was signs of a large campfire, cold and long extinguished from the looks of it, in the centre of the chamber and high above it, a naturally occurring chimney that was letting in a modicum of light, but not quite enough to illuminate all of the cavern.
As Jennings shone his torch all around the walls, he saw crude attempts at what looked a lot like some of the cave paintings he had seen discovered in certain remote areas of France painted upon them – crudely drawn stick figures supposedly meant to represent man; taller, hairier figures that could only be Sasquatch or Bigfoot; stag, rabbits, and birds.
They looked a little like something a five-year-old would draw, he thought. Or something with limited motor neurone skills.
The cave paintings, from the little Jennings could make out, all appeared to have been drawn in blood, and there were large, crimson stains all over the floor of the cavern all around him that gave off a coppery smell and made the floor sticky and tacky to the touch.
But it was what else that was in the cavern that gave him chills.
For all around the edges of the massive room he now found himself in were bones – some blatantly animal, but just as many of them visibly human.
You didn't have to be Tempe Brennan by any stretch of the imagination, he thought, to be able to recognise human tibia and fibula – not to mention ulna, humerus and rib cages – and there was no mistaking the shape of the human skull.
Some of the skulls, he noted, drawing closer, were much larger in diameter, with much bigger jaw bones and an entirely differently shaped skull – and these, he could only imagine, could only be the skulls of fellow Sasquatch the creatures must have eaten when food became scarce, heavily suggesting that as well as possessing some form of limited intellect as had always been suspected, the Bigfoot were also prone to acts of cannibalism should the need arise.

Or maybe there were different tribes, Jennings thought, *and the skulls he had found were the bones of their enemies, picked clean after their flesh had been stripped off and eaten.*
Along with the animal-like smell, there was a faint stench of decomposition but nowhere near as strong as he would have suspected, suggesting many of these bones had been here for some time.
This close to the surface, he thought, perhaps this was an old lair and the Sasquatch had abandoned it for somewhere deeper within the cave system.
He had no way of knowing for certain, and was torn about whether having discovered all this he should turn back, or carry on.
The claustrophobia he had started to feel earlier was now starting to dissipate in this much larger chamber, and Jennings thought he was slowly starting to acclimatise and get more comfortable with being underground.
Not much, just a little, but enough for him to be able to carry on a little further, should that be what he chose to do.
For the first time since being down here, Jennings wished he had brought his camera so he could get some of this on film.
He had a mobile phone - practically useless out here in Thetford Forest as a phone because of the lack of signal, and definitely of no use to him down here – but it was only a cheap model, and the camera on it was bollocks.
Any photos he tried to take of the bones down here with that piece of shit would only come out poor quality and practically undecipherable, so there was no point really even trying.
Jennings wondered where the Sasquatch were right now, and figured they must be further down the tunnels somewhere. Several fissures and openings seemed to lead off from the cavern he was in, so it looked like there were several options.
Suddenly there was a snuffling and grunting sound from somewhere up the corridor behind him, and Jennings realised with a shock that something was coming down the tunnels.
Shit, he thought. *Shit, shit, shit.*
Extinguishing his torch quickly, Jennings started to panic.
His earlier options had just been taken away from him, he realised, and now he had no choice but to continue further down the tunnels or risk being caught down here in the dark. He could always try and hide in the shadows in this cavern, he thought, but as the Sasquatch so far had largely shown themselves to be nocturnal, that probably meant they had good night vision – something backed up by the fact that they appeared to live mostly underground, and that also went some way of explaining why sightings of them were so infrequent.

The professor at the university had suggested and implied they travelled along waterways, along the various rivers and brooks and streams that ran through Thetford Forest; but from the evidence at hand, it also looked like maybe they travelled underground and the hole leading into the cave mouth he had found, back at the brook, was possibly just one of several entrances that led down here into these tunnels.

If the entrance *he* had accidentally stumbled across had remained undiscovered until now, there was absolutely no way of telling just how many more there might be hidden all the way throughout Thetford Forest.

So much of it had not been explored or mapped properly for decades, with funding to the Breckland Forestry Commission having been significantly cut these past few years thanks to the Tory government budget cuts, that all of this was entirely feasible.

Jennings thought, too, about how reluctant the authorities were to properly investigate all the missing persons cases and suspicious suicides he had uncovered over the past twenty years or so.

Was it possible the authorities knew something and were covering it up? He wondered. Maybe already knew, or at at the very least strongly suspected, that there may be Sasquatch or Bigfoot living out here in the forest?

It would certainly go some ways to explaining the lack of local media coverage over some of the disappearances in recent years he had uncovered, other than in a small regular column in the EDP called 'Weird Norfolk'; or in the sensationalist tabloid, The East Anglian and West Norfolk Explorer, which specialised in stories of UFO abductions and giant spiders rather than proper news, and had something of a shady and dubious reputation for printing unbelievable stories.

All this passed through his head in a matter of seconds.

As the heavy footsteps drew closer, Jennings hurried across the cavern – careful not to knock into any bones and create a disturbance that might alert the approaching Sasquatch to his presence – and choosing a tunnel at random, quickly darted into it.

Thankfully it was not just a fissure in the wall of the cavern, but what looked like a proper passage. Jennings readied his rifle, just in case, and stood by the entrance, waiting to see what the Sasquatch did or where it might go.

If the creature looked like it was heading this way, he would shoot it and then make a run for it back the way he had come, he thought.

He had no way of telling whether the creature was male or female, for could see no sign of any genitalia, but he could see its face and contrary to previous descriptions he had heard of the beast, it more resembled some kind of primitive primate to a bear – but obviously on a much larger and more human-like scale

than any primate he had ever seen; either in the zoo or on any of those David Attenborough programmes that always seemed to be showing on the telly somewhere.
Jennings shrank back, careful not to scrape his backpack on the tunnel walls in case it made any sound, and began watching and observing the creature. It appeared to be moving in circles around the perimeter, making sure nothing had been disturbed, before sniffing the air like a dog – no doubt trying to detect any strange or unusual smells that did not belong.
It made a noise, not a roar – more like the growl a dog would sound, possibly as a warning to any other animals – and for a second there, Jennings thought he must have been discovered...
But when another answering growl came a few seconds later, quickly Jennings realised the truth.
It wasn't a growl he was hearing, but a snore.
The Sasquatch - and there was no mistaking now that was *exactly* what this was – had only gone and fallen asleep, he thought.
Jennings started to emerge from the passage he was in, then stopped himself just in time. From the tunnel opposite to the one he was in, another Sasquatch appeared, then another, and both quickly came in and lay down, close to the first one that had originally entered the vast cavern, and promptly joined it in falling asleep.
Before long, the sounds of three Sasquatch snoring began filling the air – only amplified by the acoustics in the cavern that made the noises sound even louder than they were.
Once again, Jennings started to carefully and slowly emerge from the passage he was in, but there was a problem...
The Sasquatch were now laying directly in front of the tunnel he was in, all snuggled up together in one big, shaggy lump, meaning his only way past them was to climb over them, and no way in Hell was he about to try that anytime soon.
He didn't fancy being torn apart limb from limb like those poor animals last night, and he especially didn't like the thought of being eaten alive, which left only one other option – carrying on further down the tunnel he was in.
This tunnel, much like the cavern he had just come from, seemed to have been carved out of rock, rather than dirt like the one he had originally come down. Scrabbling around on the floor, Jennings was able to find a small piece of flint which he now used to carve an arrow in the wall, along with the letter 'r' for right, so if or when he returned this way, he would know the tunnel to the right of the main cavern would be the one he needed to take to lead him back up to the surface.

With one more last glance to make sure none of the creatures behind him were stirring, Jennings started to move down the passageway he was in. As he walked, he continued to mark more arrows on the tunnel walls with his flint to mark his progress. At some points the passage was so narrow he had to turn sideways, leading to constant fear he might get stuck at any moment, but for the most part the tunnel remained every bit as wide as the one that had brought him down here, and soon he began to make steady progress.

Several tunnels and fissures seemed to lead off from the passage he was in, but for the time being at least, Jennings chose not to take any of them - both for fear of becoming lost down here in what was essentially a rabbit warren, but also because he was curious to find out where this tunnel he was in would eventually lead.

From somewhere, presumably close by, he could hear the sound of running water – presumably only because down here sound carried and in actual fact, Jennings had no idea how close it might be. This was the exact same reason why he was very aware of where he tread, and why he was careful not to make too much sound as he walked for he had no way of knowing a) how many more Sasquatch might be down here, sleeping or otherwise, and b) when he might turn a corner and stumble across more of the creatures, or even if there were any waiting for him down any of the passages that he passed.

He stopped only once on his journey to have a piss – fearful that at any moment a Bigfoot might hear him and come to investigate, and only grateful that he had taken time that morning to empty his bowels so that at least that half was taken care of.

He had been walking for what felt like an hour when he stumbled across another massive underground cavern that turned out to be the source of the running water. In the centre of the cavern was a waterfall, and it seemed obvious that it must have been this that had produced the sounds he had been hearing for so long as the water ran into a small stream that disappeared out of the cavern through a small hole in the opposite side of the chamber.

Another tall vent, way up high in the ceiling, just like the chimney in the previous cavern he had found, produced some semblance of light and he could see both stalactites coming down from the roof, and stalagmites reaching up, that had obviously been formed at some point by the falling water.

It was a beautiful sight, and easily on a par with some of the caves that had been discovered all around the UK in places like Cheddar Gorge, and it was a wonder, Jennings thought, that no-one else had ever stumbled across the cavern before now, or if they had, survived long enough to tell the tale.

For a moment he paused, taking time to catch a breath and take in the beautiful surroundings all around him and then, thinking about the Bigfoot and Sasquatch still behind him, made the decision to push on.
He could feel a distance breeze, a down draught, that he didn't believe came from the vent high above him and by following it, Jennings hoped to eventually come back out on the surface – thus hopefully eliminating any need for him to retrace his steps and return back the way he had just come.
If he could avoid heading back to that earlier cavern with the sleeping Sasquatch inside, all the better, he thought.
There were a couple of potential passageways leading off from the cavern he currently stood in, and as he tried to contemplate and judge which of the two might be the best to move forwards, Jennings thought he heard a sound.
It sounded a little like a gentle sob, and not like any of the other sounds he had heard down here before.
It almost, he thought sounded…*human?*
Jennings held his breath for a second, and listened again.
It definitely sounded like a sob, he thought.
He took a big drink of the water, pooling in the centre of the cavern at the foot of the waterfall, and listened just one more time.
When the sound cane again, this time Jennings was able to pinpoint precisely which passage it had come from.
Marking the way he was headed on the floor of the cavern with his flint, slowly Jennings headed off in the direction of the sobs he had just heard.
A few seconds later, he found Amy Hayden…

Eleven

He found her in a small cave, just off from the main cavern.
Following the sounds of her sobs, Jennings found himself travelling down another small passage that led to another chamber not far from the cavern with the waterfall. In actual fact it was something of a wonder that he had even heard her over the sounds of the falling water, but as concentrated and focused as he was on listening out for any sound of the creatures behind him, his ears had almost become attuned to the complete silence of the caves and tunnels he was walking down, and so immediately picked up on anything out of the ordinary.
All of his senses were on high alert; he could feel the adrenaline pumping through his veins, keeping him constantly on edge, fighting the claustrophobia that was starting to build deep inside of him again, and so the sound of sobbing instantly registered as something that warranted investigating.

Amy was curled up in the far corner of the cave he found her in, laying on some furs; shivering and so disheveled he almost didn't recognise her from the missing person posters and the photographs he had seen of her. But then was it any wonder, he thought, for by now she had been missing for just a little under two months.

It was nothing short of a miracle that she was even still alive.

For a moment he stared at her as if she were an illusion, or at the very least some sort of hallucination from being down here way too long and breathing in all of this stale air, and she must have felt the same for as she looked up at him, still dressed in his Ghillie suit, she whispered in a croaky voice, "are…are you real?"

"Yes," Jennings said. "I'm real. Are you…I mean I know that it's impossible…but…is it…are you…forgive me, are you Amy Hayden?"

The woman lying there in front of him nodded.

"Have…have you come to save me?" She asked, reaching out to touch him, as though still needing to confirm to herself that he was in actual fact real.

"Are…are you here to rescue me? Where are the others? You…you need to help me. We n…n…need to get out of here. We n…n…need to escape before those…those *things* come back here.

"Frank…they k..k..killed a Frank. Butchered him. Strung him up and b…b…butchered him like a pig. They ate him. They *fucking* ate him. Made me eat him too. F…f…forced me. F…f…fed him to me. M…m…made me *eat!*

"D…d…didn't want to, but…but…but they made me. Made me *fucking eat him!*

"You have to help me," she said, visibly shaking with shock. "You need to h…h…help me get away. B…b…baby. I…n…n…need to protect my baby!"

Looking down, for the first time Jennings noted her distended belly.

"Did they…"he asked. "Did they…touch you? I mean…you know…did they…forgive me…did they…did they *rape* you?"

Amy reluctantly nodded, her shaking getting visibly worse.

"But…but…but the baby, it's not…it's not theirs. Franks. It's Franks.

"Pregnant. I was already pregnant when we came out here. T…t..three weeks.

"I was going to tell him. I was. I was going to tell Frank…it's why…why I agreed to come out here in the first place.

"I was going to tell him, I promise. You have to believe me, honest I was. I was going to tell him, but then…then all this happened.

"Those…*things*…those *fucking* things attacked us. Took us away. Dragged us down h…h…here.

"Killed Frank.

"Fucking killed Frank and *fucking ate him.*

"You...you need to help me. You need to help me get the fuck out of here.
"You need to help me escape.
"You need to help me protect my baby.
"They want my fucking baby!"
Tears and snot were running down her face as she spoke, leaving tracks down the dirt on her face, and seeing this, Jennings pulled out a handkerchief and held it out to her.
"Come on," he said. "You need to relax. You need to try and keep calm. I'm here now, and I'm going to do my best to get you out of here. But you need to stay calm, you hear me? I'm going to save you – you and the baby both – but you need to try and hold it together, do you understand? Nod if you understand me."
Amy nodded, still wiping her face with the handkerchief – by now, a very dirty shade of brown.
"Now, I need you to stay quiet, you hear me?"
Amy nodded again, sniffing.
"Good, now is there any other way out of here? We can't go back the way I came - there's Sasquatch back there and we can't get past – so we need to find another exit. Do you know where any of the other tunnels back there lead? Do you know if there's another way out at all?"
Amy carried on nodding.
"There's... there's a couple of ways out," she told him. "I tried to escape one time, got real close to the surface too, but they caught me. Smacked me around a little bit and threw me in here.
"But...but..but...I think I can find it again. I think I can show you the way. But we need to be quick. We need to move fast.
"They never sleep for long. They'll be waking up soon...and then...then they'll come for me again."
"Come on then," Jennings said. "What are we waiting for, let's move."

∗∗∗

Amy led him back the way he'd come.
Back to the cavern with the waterfall.
She started to lead him towards the passage that had originally brought him here, but Jennings stopped her.
"Not that way," he said. "The Bigfoot are back there somewhere."
She indicated the only other passage out of there.
"That way's a dead end," Amy told him. "We need to go this way. There's a few ways out from this end of the tunnels, so you show me the way you came and we'll just take one of the other passages. I've had a lot of time to explore

and unless I get too close to the surface, those *things*...Sasquatch, did you call them?" Jennings nodded. "Well, unless I get too close to one of the tunnels leading back above ground, then those creatures don't seem too bothered about stopping me."
She was starting to sound a bit more confident, he noted. A lot less frightened, and a bit more sure of herself. Her trembling had stopped, and there was a new determination about her that had been missing just a few short moments before, as though just his very presence next to her was giving her something she had been missing all this time.
Hope.
And not just hope, but reassurance – reassurance that maybe, just maybe, after all this time, everything was going to turn out to be a-okay after all.
Jennings saw her wince, and then nearly double over in pain as her hands clutched at her belly.
"Are you okay?" He asked, suddenly worried that maybe trying to get out of here with a pregnant woman in tow perhaps wasn't the brightest of ideas. "Do you need to stop and rest for a minute? Can I do anything for you?"
Amy shook her head.
"I..it's just the baby," she said. "It kicks sometimes is all. I think it reacts to my stress and as you can well imagine, I'm pretty f...fucking stressed right about now."
Is it Franks though? That's what Jennings really wanted to know. She had told him that it was; had told him that she had already been pregnant when she and her husband had come out here, but had she been?
Had she really?
She had also told him and admitted as much that the creatures down here, the Sasquatch, had touched her; sexually assaulted her; raped her.
Could it be, he wondered. *Could it possibly be that she was in denial and carrying the baby of one those things and not actually that of her dead husband?*
Could she in fact of convinced herself in her own mind that the baby was his, as a way of trying to keep him and his memory alive and in reality, was actually carrying the offspring of one those things, a little baby monster deep inside of her?
In her womb?
Except now really wasn't the time to be asking those sort of questions, Jennings told himself. Those were thoughts not even worth thinking about, let alone contemplating right now – they were things to be discussed later, after they were both out of here.
After they were safe.

"C'mon," he said. "If you're sure you're really okay, then we should probably get moving."

Jennings had no idea how long he had been down here. His watch had stopped a long time ago and he had lost all concept of time down here in the dark, but however long it had been was too long.

He wanted to be out of here.

He wanted to be out of these goddamn tunnels and more importantly, now he had located Amy Hayden, all he really wanted was to get the fuck out of Thetford Forest and never ever fucking return.

"Is that the way you came in?" Amy asked, suddenly directing his attention away from his thoughts and over to an arrow carved in the wall, pointing back the way they had just come.

Jennings nodded.

"Then we n…need to go this way," Amy said, and pulled him towards another barely visible passage in the rock opposite the wall he had marked. He had probably walked straight past it without even seeing it, it was so well concealed by the shadows, he thought. So obsessed, as he had been at the time, with finding the source of the running water – mistakenly believing that where there was running water, there might be a way out as well.

He hadn't found an exit, he thought, but *had* found the missing Amy Hayden instead, so in a way it had all worked out.

Jennings gripped her by the shoulder, and stopped her, once they had walked down the passage a little way; a small, little wave of panic suddenly threatening to take hold.

"Amy," he asked. "I hate to say this, but do you *really* know where we're headed? I mean, all of these passages all look the same. I mean, I'm not doubting you, but how are you so sure you know the way out of here?"

"I memorised it," she said. "The last time I nearly found my way out and they dragged me back here. Three of their paces to every one of mine.

"1…2…3…4…right. 1…2…3…4…5…6…second left. 1…2…3…4…5…third left. All the way ba…"

She stopped.

"*Fuck! Fuck, fuck fuck, fuck – FUCK!*" She cursed. She punched the dirt wall nearest to them with her fist.

"W…w…Wong way," she cried. "G…g…going the wrong way. Goddammit, They brought me back that way, so headed towards the surface I need to reverse the directions. *Fuck! Fuck, fuck, fuck, fuck!*

She was starting to lose it again, Jennings noted. Starting to get frustrated with herself, starting to panic and as he thought this, Jennings reached out to try and calm her down.

"Its j…just such a fucking maze down here. A fucking maze," and then, in an eerie echo of what Jennings himself had thought earlier, said, "it's like that Greek myth - you know, the one with the Minotaur. Except down here, there's more than one fucking Minotaur and there's no-one helping us get out."
She punched the wall again, harder this time.
"It's okay," he told her. "Just stop for a minute, think about it. And stop punching the wall, you'll hurt yourself."
Her knuckles were already red raw and bleeding, he saw.
"Just take a deep breath, calm yourself, and gather your thoughts."
Easy for you to say, his mind spoke up inside his head. *You don't have any idea what she's been through down here. You're lucky she's even holding it together as well as she is…*
"I know," Jennings said, and then realised he'd spoken out loud. "I know you can find us a way out," he said, pretending he'd been speaking to Amy all along. "I have faith in you, I believe in you. But I just need you to stay calm, do you understand me? Are we on the same page here?"
Amy nodded.
"Now think. Where do we have to go?"
"This way," Amy said, suddenly possessed again with a new determination. "I'm s…s…sure of it. Yes, it's this way…"
She set off again, down another passage to the left of them that sloped and appeared to be leading them further underground. "We need to g…g..go further d…d…down, before we can g…g…go back up."
She winced for a second and grabbed her stomach again, then glared at him when she caught him staring.
"I'm fine," she snapped. "I'm fine, the baby's fine, I'll just be better when we finally get the fuck out of here is all."
Won't we all? Thought Jennings.
"I'm sorry," she said. "I don't mean to snap. I'm trying, I'm really trying…"
Tears started running down her face again.
"It's okay," Jennings said. He held her close for a minute. "I can't even imagine what you must have gone through, what it must have been like for you trapped down here all this time, but we really, really need to keep going."
"I know," Any said.
She led him to another junction.
If Jennings had felt lost before, by now he had no idea where they were or where they were headed.
He only hoped Amy was right, and she *did* in fact know where they were going. She didn't appear very stable - not that he blamed her for that after all she must have endured these past two months since her disappearance – but he was very

conscious right now that by letting her take the lead, not only was he putting his own life, but also that of hers and her baby as well in her hands.
He was trusting her – trusting her to help him find a way out.
Trusting her to help them both escape.
And only time would tell whether that decision would turn out to be a mistake.
"This way…" she said, and the two of them set off once more.
From somewhere, way back in the tunnels far behind them, came the first sounds of pursuit…the Sasquatch obviously having finally discovered that Amy was no longer their prisoner.
"We need to hurry," Jennings told her, and the two of them started to increase their pace, as the sounds of pursuit behind them slowly began drawing ever closer.

Twelve

"We need to hurry," Jennings repeated, cocking his rifle and checking that it was all ready to fire should the need arise; something he expected to happen much sooner rather than later.
Because of the way that sound carried down here, Jennings had no way of knowing just how close behind them the Sasquatch were, but he didn't particularly want to find out either.
"This way," Amy told him. "No, this way - I'm s…sure of it."
"Just hold your nerve," Jennings told her. "Don't lose it on me now, we're so close to the surface now, Amy. I can feel it. Come on, I know you've got this."
This was not just him trying to bolster her confidence.
Jennings really did have a good feeling about the way they were headed.
The air was starting to smell fresher, less stale, and he was starting to feel a breeze, a draught coming from somewhere that indicated they were heading in the right direction.
Behind them, the sound of high pitched yaps, fevered growls, and snuffling sounds continued to draw closer.
As a Amy led, and Jennings followed, he kept the gun pointed back the way they'd come – ready to shoot the first Bigfoot he saw drawing close.
His nerves were almost as shot as Amy's must be right now, and he was more than prepared to shoot first, and then worry about any possible consequences later.
By now, he had more than had enough.
These Sasquatch had been a deliberate thorn in his side since the very first moment he was out here, trying to intimidate him and scare him into leaving

without finding any answers, and now Jennings was more than ready for a fight. They had pushed him so far that now, even though by rights he had invaded their territory by coming down here in the tunnels in the first place, he was more than ready to push back.

"C'mon you motherfuckers," he whispered in the silence of the tunnels. "Where are you? Come at me, motherfuckers. Come the fuck at me already."

A lot of this was false bravado, he knew.

If the Sasquatch *did* attack, Jennings was pretty sure he would shit himself, but he was dammed if he'd go down without a fight.

He had come here with the express intention of finding out what had happened to Frank and Amy Hayden and now that he had found Amy and learnt the truth, he owed it to her, he knew, to get her out of here or at the very least, hold the beasts off long enough for her to escape.

How long she might last out there in the woods on her own was another matter entirely, but then Jennings did not intend for her to be out there alone.

Sacrificing himself so she could get away was the very last option, the worst case scenario.

But he would do it in a heartbeat, he knew, if it meant that she might live.

They might be all-but-strangers, but after studying her file for so long, Jennings already felt like he knew her, knew everything about her.

"Here!" Amy led them into one last tunnel. "The way out is just round the next corner!"

They sped round the last bend, and then Jennings stopped.

Suddenly, in that moment, Jennings knew why their pursuers were not hurrying too fast down the tunnels behind them.

They had no need to.

The Sasquatch had second-guessed them and already cut off their only route of escape. One of their number was already waiting for them, and with his brethren closing in behind them, knew it was already far too late to turn around and try and find another way out…

The Sasquatch stood on both legs and beat on his chest like an angry primate. Seeing them, his prey, stood there in front of him, frozen, he let out an almighty roar.

Jennings calmly levelled his gun, aimed it, and shot the Sasquatch straight in the face – calmly because even though he was terrified, petrified in fact, he also knew all too well that if he fucked up this shot, then right here, right now, both of them were dead and he would not get another chance.

The bullet took the Sasquatch square, dead centre in the face.

Mid-roar, the Sasquatch's cry transformed into a squeal of pain.

Blood, and gore, erupted from its face where the bullet had hit, taking out part of his jaw and most of the lower half of its face.
The sound of the rifle, down here in the narrow tunnels, was deafening. Jennings ears were ringing, and he could barely hear a sound, but without hesitating he cocked the rifle and opened fire once again.
This time the Sasquatch fell, like the legendary Goliath in the bible after being beaten by David; the rest of its face destroyed, with nothing left of its features but a bloody, gory mess.
As Amy struggled over the dying corpse, Jennings attempted to push it to one side. Soon, they were both past it and heading towards the last tunnel that, hopefully, with any luck – and they could certainly do with some of that right about now, he thought - would lead them straight back up to the surface, so long as Amy's calculations were correct.
But as they turned the corner, Jennings saw another passage leading off.
"I thought you said that was the last turning," Jennings gasped, getting close now to being out of breath. He thought he was hyperventilating again, and the sooner he was out of these tunnels and breathing fresh air again, the better, he thought.
He paused to reload the rifle with ammunition from his pocket, his ears still ringing, but getting steadily better with every .
"M...must be the next one," Amy replied as they approached yet another bend in the passage. A howl came from somewhere behind them as one of the pursuing Bigfoot obviously stumbled across his fallen brother. "We're d...d...definitely getting close." She said, wincing against the pain as yet another spasm crossed her stomach.
"Come on," Jennings said, and pulled her around the last corner, swinging his rifle back to face the way they had just come. "We need to keep moving, they're getting closer."
The constant pains that Amy kept experiencing, and that caused her to almost double over in agony every time they struck, worried Jennings. It gave him great concern, and led him to believe that there might well be something wrong with the baby she was carrying. He had read her files, and knew all about the miscarriage she had suffered over a year ago, and thought the chances were fairly high she might be having another one right now.
It was hardly her fault if that *was* what was happening, he thought, but it was the last thing either of them needed right now, especially with those *things* breathing down their neck and about to close in on them at any second.
It was specifically for this reason that Jennings hoped that he was wrong. The timing quite literally couldn't have been worse.

Even if they *did* somehow manage to escape these tunnels, they still had to get out of the forest – potentially with the Sasquatch right behind them at every step - and Jennings already didn't fancy their chances, trying to cross all that way with a pregnant woman in tow. But if he was right, and she was having a miscarriage, that only complicated matters further.

The best he could hope for, he thought, was for him to try and keep the Sasquatch busy, and take down as many of their number as he could, while Amy fled the forest, but Jennings was no fool and knew, the odds were certainly not in *either* of their favours.

Even if he *could* keep the Sasquatch busy and distracted long enough for Amy to make her escape, Jennings doubted that she would be able to make it out the forest on her own and so was already pretty much resigned to the fact that, chances were, at least one of them, if not both, was going to die tonight.

He would do everything in his power to stop that from happening, but if he *was* going to go down, he thought, then by God he would go down fighting.

And if his death meant poor Amy Hayden got to survive, then at least he would die knowing his death had been worthwhile.

But first, he thought, they had still had to get out of these *fucking* tunnels or else neither of them would stand a chance.

"Shit! Shit, shit, shit, shit, shit!"

Still pointing his rifle back the way they'd come, Jennings turned back to Amy.

"What is it? What's wrong?" He demanded.

The small cavern they had emerged into had a single tunnel leading off from it, that sloped upwards towards a hole leading back to the surface, but it would be a tight fit getting Amy through, he saw. It could *probably* be done, Jennings thought, but it would certainly be a close thing, and he would probably have to go up there first and widen the hole if they were both going to escape that way. Otherwise there was the very real danger that she might get stuck halfway through and after all he – *they* – had been through already, there was no way, he thought, that he was about to just up and abandon her.

Not having already come this far…

"I thought I remembered this way being bigger," Amy cursed. She began punching the tunnel walls again, until Jennings reached over, grabbed her fist, and stopped her.

"It looks as like there might have been a collapse here at some point," he said, pointing up towards the narrow hole. The walls here were dirt again, not rock, and looked like they had only recently been disturbed.

He glanced back the way they'd come.

They were running out of time, he thought. They had no more than a couple of minutes at best before the Sasquatch got past their fallen comrade, judging from

the whoops and growls coming from the tunnels far behind them, and it was too late to now to turn around and try and find another way out.
Which meant the only option left to them was forwards.
He had no way of knowing just how many Bigfoot were coming down the tunnels after them, but quickly decided it didn't matter anyway.
Whatever happened, if they didn't get the fuck out of here right now, then both of them were screwed.
"Amy, Amy, listen to me. Do you hear me?"
She nodded.
"We can't go back, those *things* are way too close, do you understand?" He asked her.
Amy nodded again.
"Listen to me, listen to me. This is our only chance, we can only go forward, do you understand? This is the only way – the *only* way. If we go back, those things will get us.
"I need to go up there first; I need to widen the hole so I can pull you through behind me, you get me? I'm not abandoning you, and I need you to stay close, okay? Stay right behind me and everything will be okay, I promise.
"I came here to rescue you, and that's exactly what I'm going to do, okay?
"I'm going to get you out of here, I promise."
Jennings turned and quickly ascended the small slope. He had to get down on his hands and knees for some of it, and felt himself slip a couple of times in the loose dirt as he did so, but Amy had obviously listened to him and was close behind, he noted.
Good girl…
The sounds of the pursuing Sasquatch behind them suddenly increased as he reached the top of the slope, and began to try and widen the hole digging away at the dirt and soil; conscious at every moment that the clock was ticking against them. Thankfully the dirt gave way easily, and it didn't look like it would take much, Jennings thought, before the hole in front of him would be wide enough to admit them both.
Suddenly, behind him, Amy screamed and turning his head, Jennings saw a couple of the Sasquatch had a hold of Amy and were starting to pull her back the way that they'd just come.
"GET OFF HER," he shouted at them. "GET THE FUCK OFF HER!"
He tried to aim the rifle back down the tunnel towards the creatures, but there wasn't exactly enough room up here for him to manoeuvre and what's more, Jennings was worried about accidentally hitting Amy even if he *did* manage to open fire.

He started to crawl backwards down the passage after her, even as one of the Sasquatch started to climb back up to meet him – coming after *him,* this time, not her.

As he levelled his rifle at the creature, now virtually on top of him - so close he could smell its foul, fetid breath that stank of carrion and rotting flesh – he attempted to fire his rifle, but the creature, the Sasquatch, batted it away at the last minute so instead of hitting the monster in front of him, his shot went wild and buried itself in the roof, sending dirt and soil down on top of him.

As the rifle fell out of his grasp and started sliding down the steep slope he was on, Jennings reached for his belt and pulled out the large hunting knife he always kept there instead. Without so much as a second thought, Jennings thrust the knife, as hard, and with as much strength as he could possibly muster, upwards and into the attacking Sasquatch. He heard the monster let out a surprised grunt of pain as it felt the knife entering, and then an almighty squeal as Jennings dragged the sturdy blade violently across, ripping open the creature's belly.

Jennings felt the beast's hot, warm blood come flooding out – along with most of its insides - making him retch not just at the sensation of the creature's guts and intestines spilling out all over him, but also at the smell. Thick, black blood gushed out from the creature's mouth - splattering him in the face – even as the great big, massive beast went into its death throes, collapsed and then promptly died right there on top him.

For the big bastards that they were, Jennings thought, all in all they were a helluva lot easier to kill than he ever would have thought.

But the battle wasn't over yet.

They still had Amy.

Pushing the monster off of him and sliding with it down to the bottom of the slope, Jennings picked up his rifle again, took aim, and then fired at the big, bad motherfucker doing its best to try and drag Amy away. The bullet clipped the big beast in the arm.

Amy was putting up a hell of a struggle, he saw, and fighting the creature every step of the way, but there was no way that the Sasquatch was ever letting her go. Jennings reloaded his gun, waited a moment until he had a clear shot, and then opened fire again as the beast angrily turned to face him, baring its teeth and letting out an almighty roar.

This time Jennings aim was more true, and his shot took the Sasquatch directly in it's eye – causing the creature to let out an almighty howl as it collapsed, part of its brain spraying up the wall behind it as the bullet exited through the back of its skull.

Jennings could hear the sounds of even more of the Bigfoot coming down the tunnels behind them, and gripped Amy by the arm.
"COME ON!" He told her. "We need to get out of here, NOW!"
The two of them awkwardly clambered back up the slope towards the exit leading back out to the surface.
There was no time to dig anymore, Jennings thought. He would just have to let Amy go first and hope the hole he'd tried to enlarge was now big enough for her to get through.
He gripped Amy's arm and made to push her in front of him.
Something crossed in front of the hole leading back to the surface, momentarily blocking out the light, and for a split second, Jennings briefly thought someone must have come looking for him out here, and that the two of them were both now saved…but then he saw the shape of the hairy figure stood out there, in front of the only exit currently available to them, and in a wave of horror, instantly realised the truth.
That wasn't another person out there, come to save them, it was yet another Sasquatch…the supposedly 'dumb' creatures had once more outthought him once again, and cut off his only means of escape.
No, Jennings thought, cursing both himself and the situation he now found himself in. *So close! We were so so close! We so almost made it out of here! We almost got away – we almost escaped!*
Jennings smacked his fist against the dirt wall in frustration, before carefully manoeuvring his rifle forwards and opening fire at the creature blocking his path.
The Sasquatch let out a howl as the bullet tore through it.
The sound of the gun in such a small space threatened to bring more of the roof down on top of him, as soil and dirt started to rain down on Jennings, but for the briefest of seconds, the way ahead was clear.
He started to push forwards, still dragging Amy, even as the now wounded Sasquatch returned, back to his position just outside the tunnel entrance.
Whatever damage Jennings's shot had done had obviously not been fatal, for instead of killing or mortally wounding the creature, all he seemed to have done was piss it off, Jennings suddenly realised.
Up at the tunnel entrance just ahead of him, the injured Sasquatch began roaring, stomping and thumping on the outside of the tunnel; bringing its fists down heavily as it did so, causing more soil and dirt to fall on Jennings as all around him, the tunnel he and Amy were both in suddenly started to collapse.
He felt Amy's hand being snatched out of his grasp and looking back, the last thing Jennings saw was her being pulled away, kicking and screaming, back down the tunnels they had just come, by three of the pursuing Bigfoot, just as

the walls and the ceiling all around him started to come down on top of him, essentially burying him alive.

The last thing Jennings had a chance to think, just before the tunnel finally caved in on him, was '*I'm sorry, Amy. I tried. I really tried to get you out, but I failed you. I'm sorry...*'

And then everything all went black...the sound of Amy's screams still ringing in his ears, even as the tunnel collapsed on him.

Thirteen

It was almost three full days before anyone came looking for Detective Inspector Chris Jennings and by that time, the camera he had left behind, hanging from a tree for those who came after him to find, had been fully exposed to the elements.

Because of all the cold and frost the past few days that had penetrated the video camera and damaged its insides, any footage Jennings might have previously shot had been rendered effectively useless, meaning anything he'd filmed was now essentially lost for good.

There was no way of telling what might have happened to Detective Inspector Chris Jennings, and no way of telling where he might possibly have gone.

All anyone knew for certain was that something must have occurred for him to abandon all his stuff.

What that *something* might have been though was still very much open to conjecture...

***

The Police Search and Rescue team had been searching for three days when they eventually decided to give up.

By then Jennings had been missing for almost ten days.

They had focused their search mainly in and around the area Jennings' colleague had directed him to where, during a previous search for the missing campers, Frank and Amy Hayden, search dogs had begun acting nervous.

This time around the dogs had appeared fine, and seemed much better behaved and easier to control, but so far had contributed very little of any use to the investigation into Jennings' apparent disappearance.

Their attention had briefly been drawn towards what looked like a small animal burrow, half-buried and concealed under the roots of a fallen tree on the banks of a babbling brook down here in the gully, but despite evidence it had only recently been filled – no doubt by subsidence – there had been no other indication it had anything to do with their case, or where Jennings might possibly have gone.

It was the last day of the search.

Detective Superintendent Matthew Collins was overseeing the close down of the investigation, having taken a special interest in Jennings' case.

Also in attendance was a young Detective Constable named Jensen, and the last of the Search and Rescue team.

"Looks like we can chalk up yet another one to The Norfolk Files," the Detective Superintendent said to the last of the Search and Rescue officers.

Young Jensen looked on, confused.

"Norfolk Files?" He asked, puzzled.

"Consider then a bit like The X-Files," Detective Superintendent Collins told him. "But with no Fox Mulder to investigate them. It's where unexplained and unsolved cases go to die. A bit like the Slush pile in a newspaper office – you know, the place where they always file big cat sightings, or UFO sightings, or alien abductions, that sort of thing, ready to pull out on a slow news day.

"The Norfolk Files is where we file anything inexplicable, or anything mysterious we can't otherwise explain.

"Yes, yes, I know," the Superintendent continued. "I know exactly what you are going to say – Thetford isn't in Norfolk, it's Suffolk, but that doesn't matter.

"The Norfolk Files is just what we call the place where we store such cases.

"We've got cases from Cambridgeshire and as far away as Lincolnshire there in the files too. Most of them though are from Norfolk, hence the name."

"So you're just going to give up?" Jensen asked. "Just not going to bother looking for Jennings out here any more?"

"Son," the Superintendent said. "We have nothing more to go on. We know D.I Jennings came out here, yes, and we know he came this way – hence why we discovered all his stuff out here, abandoned – but other than that, we have nothing further to pursue. No more clues. Nor any indication where he might possibly have headed off to next.

"He has no immediate family to speak of, was no more than an average police officer at best, and was known for being a bit odd, a little weird, and obsessed with these woods, but without anything further to go on, I don't see we have any other choice but to close the case, at least for now.

"Im sorry, but I simply cannot afford to invest any more manpower into this investigation right now. As you well know, there is a budget coming up and I'm afraid, much as I'd like to, I simply cannot justify spending any more time, money, energy or resources on this right now, especially without even the slightest hope of having something conclusive to show for it all at the end of it."

"So you're just going to give up?" Jensen continued, insistent, determined to get some kind of definitive answer from his boss. "You're really *not* going to keep on searching – even though it's blatantly obvious something must have happened to Detective Inspector Jennings out here?"

"Not right now, no," his superior reluctantly conceded. "If there are any new developments, of course we will not hesitate to reopen the case, but I find the chances of that happening highly unlikely.

"I've been working out this way and around these parts for a long time, son, and let me tell you, there's something very *wrong* about this forest. Something very *wrong* about much of the woodland in and around this area in fact.

"More people disappear or get lost out here every year than are ever officially reported, and all sorts of phenomena are alleged to have occurred out here over the last thirty years or so – from missing time, to strange lights in the trees, to compasses and electrical equipment playing up, and that's not even mentioning the absurd claims that some kind of Bigfoot lives out here somewhere.

"There's even a rumour that the British Army know all about the kind of things that go on out here, and that's why a big part of the forest is out of bounds.

"Not because they practice using live ammunition out here, but because they are secretly investigating some of the strange phenomena alleged to go on in these parts.

"It's all rubbish, I know. Conspiracy theories and such like, but there's no denying strange things *do* happen out here, so it does make you think.

"But sometimes you just have to accept that there are no explanations for some of the stuff that happens out here, and that's why we have The Norfolk Files.

"So that we have a written record of all that goes on out here, even if most times we have no explanation for any of it all.

"Honestly, you want my advice? When it comes to some of the strange things that go on around here, you're probably better off not thinking about it too much. You start looking into it all, start examining things too closely, honestly it'll drive you mad.

"Look at the case of the missing D.I Jennings for example. He started getting obsessed with everything that goes on out here, started delving too deep into things best left alone, and look what happened to him."

"But that's the point. We don't know what happened to Jennings…" the Young Detective Constable insisted.

"Precisely," the Detective Superintendent said and wrapping his arm around the boy's shoulders, started to lead him back up the gully, closely followed by the last of the Search and Rescue team.

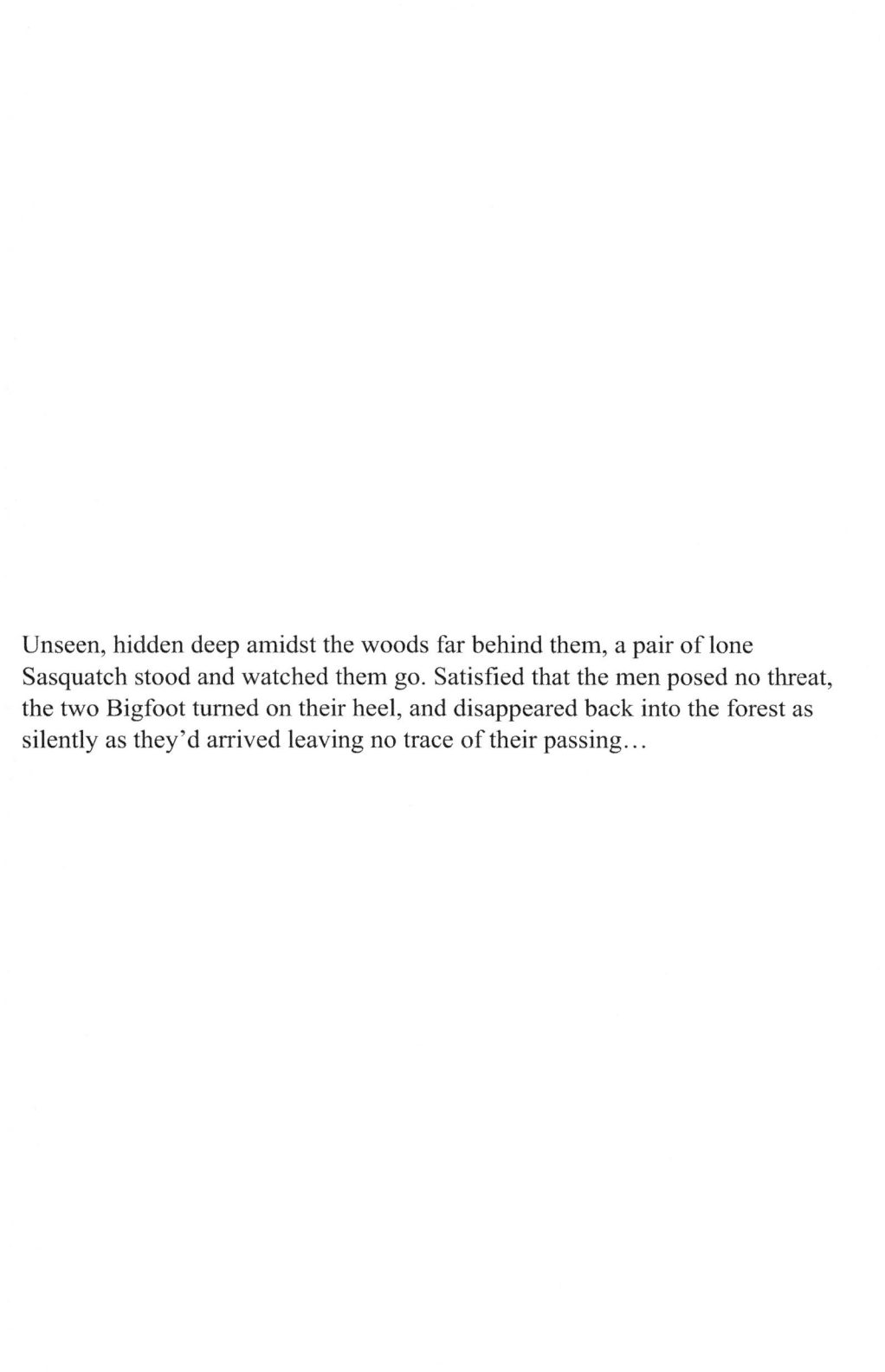

Unseen, hidden deep amidst the woods far behind them, a pair of lone Sasquatch stood and watched them go. Satisfied that the men posed no threat, the two Bigfoot turned on their heel, and disappeared back into the forest as silently as they'd arrived leaving no trace of their passing…

Read on for an exclusive first look at the next chilling chapter in The Norfolk Files…

The Grishnakka by Mark Woods
(The Norfolk Files book two)

"Have either of you ever heard of The Grishnakka?"
Robin and Jeremy both looked over at their friend where he sat on the other side of the campfire and together, both shook their heads; the light from the flames the only thing illuminating their faces in the darkness that surrounded them.
"No," Jeremy said at long last, when it became blatantly apparent their friend, Gary, was not about to elaborate. "What's a 'Grishnakka'?"
Robin, Gary, and Jeremy were all Boy Scouts – or at least, they had been up until a few days ago. Whether they still were or not after this summer still remained to be seen.
They were supposed to have been off camping with the rest of their Boy Scout Pack this weekend. But after getting busted lighting firecrackers and throwing them at some of their fellow scouts a few days ago, they had been non-too-politely told in no uncertain terms by their Akela that they were no longer welcome on the trip and not only that, but that their continued membership in the Scouts was something that would have to be discussed upon the pack's return.
Robin, Gary, and Jeremy's parents had all paid good money for the trip and so, knowing that their parents would be furious when they learnt that the boys were no longer going – let alone, the reason for their exclusion in the first place – the boys had simply elected not to tell them.
Instead, the three boys had decided, they would still go camping; they would just go camping on their own.
It had been Gary's idea to camp up here by the old abandoned quarry - well away from the official Boy Scout Campsite that lay several miles away, over to the west somewhere - and though entry to the quarry and its surrounding area was strictly forbidden, Gary had assured them he knew of a secret path leading up here, by way of a hole in the fence that marked the perimeter.
Jeremy had had his doubts about coming up here, not least because he didn't want to get himself into any more trouble, but he had eventually been talked round by Gary and Robin when they had taken it in turns to call him 'a pussy.'
And now, here they were.
Miles from town, miles from anywhere in fact, with no-one any the wiser of where they actually were.
Their Akela, as Boy Scout leaders were always addressed in some kind of bizarre homage to the Jungle Book, thought they were at home; their parents

thought the three boys were with the rest of the Boy Scouts – it was, or so Gary explained, a victimless crime. And by the time this weekend was over, he told them, no doubt their Boy Scout Leader would have calmed down and rethought his decision to permanently exclude them as well.

Jeremy wasn't so sure.

He had seen how mad Akela had been, had seen the expression on his face and had his doubts, but Gary was convinced that he could talk the Boy Scout Leader around and once Gary got an idea in his head, there was no talking him out of it. And so, at Gary's behest, the three of them had packed up their camping gear, ridden their bikes all the way up here to the quarry and now, here they sat, outside their tents, gathered around a makeshift campfire, toasting marshmallows whilst staring up at the stars.

"So, now we're up here, what are we supposed to do now?" Robin had asked, once they'd set up their tents.

The quarry was flooded, and had been for years, and was a great place to swim – though access to the quarry had long been prohibited due to several teenagers who had disappeared up here during the late Seventies and early Eighties, presumably drowned though no-one had ever discovered their bodies – but none of them were about to go swimming in the dark.

That was just asking for trouble.

With more than a few hours left to go until sunrise, Gary instead had come up with a different idea.

"How about we each tell each other scary stories?" he suggested.

"I don't know any spooky stories," Robin said, and both boys looked at Jeremy.

"I don't know any scary stories either," he told them, though in truth this was a bit of a lie.

He *did* actually know a couple of scary stories, it was true, but he was not in any kind of rush to repeat them for fear the other two boys might find them a bit 'babyish', and then use them to take the piss out of him again.

"What about you, seeing as how it was your bright idea?" Jeremy retaliated. "Surely you must have a scary story or two up your sleeve…"

And that was when Gary had asked them both if they'd ever heard of 'The Grishnakka'…

***

"So, come on then, what's a Grishnakka when it's at home?" Robin asked now, echoing the same question Jeremy himself had just asked, just a few short moments ago.

"Well, you see, that's the thing," Gary said, answering them both now, even as he scooted a little bit closer to the fire. "That's the thing, you see; *no-one really knows...*"
He paused for a second, for dramatic effect.
There was a bit of a chill to the air now that the sun had gone down and though it was still warm, a cool breeze was blowing up here by the quarry.
Gary pulled out another marshmallow, stuck it on a stick, and began to slowly toast it over the fire.
"You see, according to local legend, no-one who has ever seen 'The Grishnakka' is ever supposed to have lived to tell the tale," he said, turning his stick slowly back and forth in an attempt to toast his marshmallow evenly. "But people have heard it, up here by the quarry, and it is said that it gets its name from the noise that it makes whilst tracking down its prey..."
And with this, Gary proceeded to gently click both his top and his bottom sets of teeth together until he started to make a kind of clacking sound – a bit like someone grinding their teeth, or the kind of noise you might expect to hear if someone's teeth were chattering because they were cold...
"*Grishnakka-nakka-nakka-nakka-nakka...*" he went, and both boys listening to him fought hard to suppress a shiver at the sound. "*Grishnakka-nakka-nakka-nakka-nakka....*
"It is said," Gary continued, "that just the sight of this creature is enough to drive a grown man insane, and that 'The Grishnakka' is the real reason they shut down the quarry all those decades ago, and then flooded it into the bargain. "It is also whispered, in secret circles around town by those in the know, that 'The Grishnakka' is the real reason for all those teenage disappearances that happened, way back in the Seventies and Eighties."
"I thought they all drowned," Jeremy said, at least that was what his parents had told him when they'd warned him off ever coming up here a few years ago.
"That's just what they *want* you to think," Gary replied. "Truth is, they never found any of the bodies – *not a single one.*"
"Bullshit, I call bullshit," Robin said, and shook his head in disbelief. "They never found any of the bodies because the quarry is so deep."
"That's what they say," Gary admitted. "But then, *they* would say that if they didn't want anyone to ever find out the truth, wouldn't they?"
"Who's this *'they'*?" Jeremy asked, suddenly weighing in. "And if people only ever talk about this *'Grishnakka'* in secret circles, how come *you* know about it? And how come neither of us have ever heard any mention of it before now?"
"Because my dad is the local Chief Constable," Gary said, a fact he never once failed to mention at any given opportunity. "I overheard him one night, talking to the Mayor and several of the town's leading businessmen at an unofficial

Council meeting being held at my house, late one night, long after I was supposed to have been in bed. Mum was at one of her Mother's meetings the local townswomen always hold from time-to-time, and I was thirsty and in need of a drink and had snuck downstairs when I heard them talking.

"They were discussing the quarry, and talking about how no-one had seen or heard anything of *The Grishnakka*' in almost a decade now, and how it might be in the town's best interests to drain and re-open the quarry.

"My dad and the Mayor were the only two dead set against it.

"They still remembered what had happened all those years ago when those teenagers disappeared. Those in favour of re-opening the quarry were all new-comers to the town, who had all moved here in the years since the disappearances and so did not really believe any of the stories they'd heard of *The Grishnakka*', whispered behind closed doors, and thought them no more than just another urban myth, or local legend.

"I kind of got the impression - from where I stood, hid behind the door to my dad's study - that in truth, they were merely humouring my dad and the Mayor, but it did not take long for both men to set them straight.

"They told the other Councilmen, in no uncertain terms, exactly why they thought it was a bad idea – no a *terrible* idea – to re-open the quarry, but the businessmen refused to listen, right up until my dad and the Mayor started recounting the story of '*The Grishnakka*' and began telling them exactly what it was they were dealing with.

"When both men were finally done, all the businessmen went silent.

"Only one businessman still refused to believe and told the Mayor and my dad that his mind was made up, and that he was headed up to the old quarry in the morning to appraise the land and assess exactly how much it was worth, but the next day he disappeared and no-one ever saw or heard anything of him again.

"And after that, strangely enough, all the other Councilmen suddenly dropped the idea of re-opening the quarry.

"All that was about six months ago, and that was the first and last time I ever heard my dad talking about '*The Grishnakka*'..."

"I remember that businessman disappearing," Robin said, suddenly speaking up. "Didn't they find his car up on one of the back roads leading up here a few days later, after he vanished, all abandoned? And didn't they, like, say he had some kind of financial problems or something, and that the most likely thought was that he must have come up here to commit suicide by throwing himself into the quarry?"

"Yeah, that's right," Jeremy said. "I remember that too. Didn't they say he had major money problems or something that he'd been keeping secret all this time? And that the Inland Revenue or some shit were after him, and were

investigating him for fraud or tax evasion, or some kind of money-laundering or something from back when he lived down in London?"
"That was the official story people put around, yes," Gary said. "But what I heard was that was all just a cover story my dad and the Mayor put around to add credibility to the suicide story. And that the missing businessman had never had any kind of tax problems before he came up here. All that stuff about the Inland Revenue, tax evasion, and money laundering? It was all just made up by the Mayor and my dad."
"Fuckkkk…" Robin said. "Like some kind of big conspiracy…and all to keep The Grishnakka's existence a secret."
"Bullshit," Jeremy said and stood up, kicking another log towards the fire. "Gary, you are so full of shit! You're nothing but a liar, man; a great big stinking liar. There's no way your dad would be involved in anything like that. I've met him – he's a good man, an honest man. Why else would he have received that big commendation last year? There's no way on earth he'd ever be involved in some kind of big cover-up, let alone any kind of conspiracy, if he thought for a moment someone prominent in town had been murdered."
"You don't know him like I do," Gary said. "All you see is a good man, an honest man – and that's true, he is, he takes his job very seriously – but he's also a man who wants the best for this town. Is obsessed with protecting it and everyone who lives here in it, and sometimes such an obsession makes a man to do desperate things."
"Gary, you are so full of shit," Jeremy repeated. He turned and stalked off towards the trees lining the top of the quarry, the light from his mobile phone the only thing lighting his way. The only thing it was good for up here, because one of the first things they'd noticed as soon as they'd started setting up camp was that any kind of phone signal up here was virtually non-existent.
"Seriously, you must think I'm really stupid if you actually think I believe you. There's no way there's any such thing as *'The Grishnakka'*. Admit it, you just made it up – because if there really was such a thing, you'd think at least one of us would of heard about it before now."
"Where are you going?" Robin asked, sounding worried. "I don't think any of us should really be going off on our own."
"I'm going to go have a piss, if that's alright with you," Jeremy said, snapping back at Robin; more than a little pissed off that his friend had bought Gary's story so readily. "Unless you want to come with me and shake it for me, of course?"
He was starting to seriously think it had been a mistake to come up here, camping with his friends, let alone lying to his parents by omission about their possible future exclusion from the Scouts. In fact, the more he thought about it,

the more coming up here was beginning to look less and less like it had been a good idea.
It was all Gary's fault they were here in the first place.
It had been his idea to come up here, his firecrackers they'd thrown, and his bright idea to ambush their fellow Scouts whilst they were supposed to be out on patrol, orienteering and learning to read a compass correctly.
"Just don't wander too far from camp," Gary shouted out behind him. "We don't want to have to come find you, and while you're there – keep an ear out for The Grishnakka. You know what they say – you always hear him before you see him, but by the time he finds you, it's already far too late…"
Jeremy flipped him the bird and just carried on walking.
"I told you, there's no such thing as The Grishnakka," he said, not entirely sure who he was trying to convince. The closer he got to the tree-line, the more likely Gary's story suddenly began to sound – but that was just because it was dark, Jeremy reasoned.
Scary stories always sounded more believable in the dark.
Jeremy disappeared in amongst the trees…

***

"Do you think he'll be alright?" Robin asked, watching him go. "I'm a bit worried about him – what if he goes too far and ends up falling into the quarry in the dark?"
"He'll be fine," Gary said, sticking another marshmallow on the end of his long pointy stick. "He's a big boy, I'm sure he can handle himself.
"As long as The Grishnakka doesn't get him that is…"

***

Jeremy stalked off into the darkness of the trees.
Gary really had annoyed him, he thought. First by bringing them up here where they shouldn't even be, persuading him to come by calling him a pussy, and then by telling them that stupid story and convincing Robin it was real.
Of course there was no such thing as The Grishnakka, he thought. In a small town like this, it was impossible to keep such a thing a secret, and if there were a monster up here in the woods then someone, someone, would surely have mentioned it before now.
Stupid, fucking prick, Jeremy thought. He didn't know why he always seemed to hang around with Gary all the time – it wasn't as if he had a shortage of people wanting to be his friend after all. If he ever thought seriously about it, Jeremy guessed he just hung around with Gary because in a way he kind of felt sorry for him. As the local Chief Constable's son, people were less inclined to

be friends with Gary – namely because they were always worried Gary might snitch on them, or rat them out to his dad if they did anything wrong or upset him – and this in turn had led Gary to start to rebel and play up; overcompensating Jeremy supposed, until people began to regard him as something of a bad influence.

Robin was what could only be described as being a bit 'slow'- not autistic, not retarded, or Asperger's or anything, but just a little bit less bright and articulate than most other kids his age. He was easily led, and this was one of the reasons why *he* had first started hanging out with Gary – because just like his friend, he too was regarded as something of an outsider by the rest of their peer group, and found it difficult to make other friends.

Jeremy had a whole lot of other options open to him, it was true, but he also thought a small part of him also got off from hanging around with Gary because if there was one thing you could always count on, it was that life was never dull with Gary around.

At least not for long…

Mind you, Jeremy thought, that wasn't always necessarily a good thing. Sometimes there was a lot to be said for a quiet life.

Jeremy looked around him.

Lost in his thoughts, he suddenly realised he had walked a lot further than he'd meant to. Oh well, he was here now – and he was sure he'd be able to find his way back if he just retraced his steps.

Jeremy pulled out his cock and started to piss. A warm stream of urine began to splatter the local fauna, and Jeremy closed his eyes and let out a comforting sigh as he embraced the feeling of immense satisfaction at finally being able to empty his bladder after sitting on it for so long.

A sound in the bushes from behind him stopped him mid-flow.

There was something there, he thought. Moving about behind him, hidden by the darkness and the trees.

Gary.

"Gary?" Jeremy said. "Robin? If that's either of you, you'd better stop fucking around. Can't a guy even have a piss in peace without you two couple of jokers pissing them about?"

He felt his bladder relax again, as a warm stream of urine once more started to flow. He was just about finished, and just about to shake, when the sound came again.

Grishnakka-nakka-nakka-nakka-nakka-nakka-nakka….

"Seriously you guys, just pack it the fuck in. You're not even funny," Jeremy said, getting angry again now. "You're not scaring me, you know," he said and turned, zipping himself back up.

Something impossibly tall, and white, and made entirely from the bones of its victims – all claws, and teeth, and fangs, and talons – leapt out of the bushes at him and attacked poor Jeremy before he could react, barely even giving him a chance to scream.
Grishnakka-nakka-nakka-nakka-nakka-nakka, the creature clacked, as it proceeded to tear poor Jeremy apart.
Grishnakka-nakka-nakka-nakka-nakka-nakka...

***

"What was that?" Robin suddenly asked, hearing something - what sounded like some sort of scream - coming from far off behind them, back amongst the treeline. "Was that a scream? Did you just hear a scream? I'm sure I just heard a scream. Do you think it was Jeremy? Do you think he's in trouble? Do you think The Grishnakka got him?"
"There is no Grishnakka," Gary said. "I made it all up, Jeremy was right. It was just a bit of fun, a joke, you know?
"None of it was real. The Grishnakka doesn't exist."
"I definitely heard a scream," Robin insisted.
"Probably an animal," Gary said, and went back to toasting his marshmallows, even though he was starting to feel a little bit sick now from already eating so many of them.
There was another noise in the night.
A crashing sound, like something big moving through the trees.
A deer maybe, Gary thought. *Or maybe...maybe it* was *The Grishnakka...*
The noise came again, but different this time.
This time, it sounded a little bit like...
Grishnakka-nakka-nakka-nakka-nakka....
Robin turned visibly pale, even by the light of the campfire.
"If that's the case," he said, "then what the actual fuck was that? Did you hear *that*? Please tell me you heard that..."
"Probably just Jeremy messing about," Gary said, but even *he* was starting to sound a little bit worried now, Robin noted. "He's just fucking with us is all - trying to get his own back on me for spooking him with that stupid story."
Grishnakka-nakka-nakka-nakka-nakka...
The sound came again.
Closer now, but still in the trees, out of sight.
"It's just Jeremy," Gary repeated, but even to himself he didn't sound all that convinced.

"Jeremy? Jeremy, is that you?" Robin asked, calling out. He got to his feet, and started moving towards the tree-line in the direction the sound was coming from.
Closer to the sound, even as it came again…
Grishnakka-nakka-nakka-nakka-nakka…
"No…no, Robin, don't…" Gary said, now less convinced than ever that it was Jeremy out there, messing about in the trees. "Robin, get back here…stay here by the campfire."
Gary got up to his feet as well, trying desperately to remember everything his dad and the Mayor had said about The Grishnakka that night when he had eavesdropped on their conversation, even as he started moving forwards – closer to Robin – so he could pull his friend back, away from the trees.
"Robin, I mean it…get away from the trees…" Gary started to say, but already it was far too late.
Something white, seemingly made entirely of bone, and all teeth, and claws, and talons and fangs, dropped from the trees and straight onto Robin even as he started screaming. Before Gary's very eyes, the *thing*…whatever it was – *The Grishnakka,* his mind screamed at him, *it had to be The Grishnakka, for what else could it be* – tore his friend apart, sending blood, and entrails, and pieces of his insides flying; splattering Gary where he stood, watching, frozen in fear at the scene being played out before him, unable to move where he was rooted to the spot.
For a single second, Gary just stood there – then his fight or flight response kicked in and Gary turned and fled.
"Oh fuck, oh fuck, oh fuck, oh fuck, oh fuck…" Gary muttered as he ran, feeling his bladder starting to let go. Warm urine flowed down his legs, soaking his jeans. *"Not real, not real, not real, not real…"*
The Grishnakka was not real, he told himself. It was just a story, something his dad had made up. It couldn't be here now, killing his friends, it just couldn't…
Except, that wasn't exactly true, was it?
He thought again about the night he had heard his dad and the Mayor talking. In the months since that conversation he'd overheard that night, Gary had managed to convince himself that his dad and the Mayor must have known he was there all along, and just told the story to wind him up and spook him – knowing he was there all the time, listening in behind the door.
The next morning, over breakfast, his dad had winked at him and asked if he'd had a good night's sleep the night before with a knowing glint in his eye, almost like the two of them were sharing a private joke.

And then, in a jovial manner that was most unlike him, said, "I hope me and the other Councilmen didn't keep you up late last night with all our talking. We got into quite a heated discussion at one point..." and winked at him again.
"Have a nice day, dear," Gary's mum had said after that, "and remember, stay safe," and then she had kissed her husband and walked him out to his car, and then that was that.
Gary had tried to forget about The Grishnakka after that, tried to pretend he had never heard anything that night.
But then he had started hearing the whispers amongst some of the people in town when they thought no-one was in earshot, amongst people he thought he knew, and whose children he had grown up alongside, and had seen their furtive glances towards him when they realised he was listening, and had known at least some of that story he'd heard that night must be true.
But that couldn't be right, surely?
The story he'd heard couldn't possibly be true…
Monsters didn't exist, they weren't real…everyone knew that.
And that, that was the real reason why Gary had brought himself and his friends up here in the first place tonight. Why, when the opportunity had presented itself, Gary had suggested he and his friends come up here to the quarry for their illicit camping trip, and why he had then shared with them the story of The Grishnakka.
Because he had wanted to prove to himself that the stories he'd heard, whispered in quiet corners, weren't true – that there was no such thing as The Grishnakka – but also because he'd been too scared to come up here on his own.
A decision he was now starting to regret.
Both his friends were now dead, and all because of him, and unless he moved fast, it looked like he was in very real danger of being next.
It was only as he finally hit the road, leading away from the quarry and back down to town, that Gary suddenly remembered his bike.
Though the boys had originally used their bikes to get up here earlier, in his panic, Gary had left his back there, up at the campsite.
Gary cursed himself.
On foot, he knew, he stood no chance of outrunning The Grishnakka…but on a bike…if he'd have only thought of that, instead of just blindly turning and running, then he might now have stood more chance of getting away.
Too late now, he thought.
No way was he turning back, not now, no way.
That would be suicide, he thought.
No, his best chance, Gary figured, was just to keep running and hopefully if he could just stay ahead of the monster pursuing him for a just little while longer –

say, until he reached town or, at the very least, its outskirts - then, with any luck, The Grishnakka might eventually grow tired of the chase and end up turning around and just heading back to the quarry.
All he had to do, he thought, *was just keep...on...running...*
Suddenly, the sound Gary had heard earlier, back up at camp, sounded again - but this time in front of him instead of from behind.
Grishnakka-nakka-nakka-nakka-nakka...
For a moment, Gary thought he must have somehow gotten turned around in the dark and was now accidentally heading back the way he'd come, back towards the quarry, but then, with a shock, he suddenly realised the truth.
The monster, the creature, whatever it was, was really that fast.
Somehow The Grishnakka had managed to get ahead of him.
Grishnakka-nakka-nakka-nakka-nakka came the sound again…but this time, before Gary could even think about turning around and fleeing, the creature was upon him; ripping out his guts and eviscerating him, even as it tore him apart.
The last thing Gary saw, just before he died, was The Grishnakka standing over him and then…then there was nothing.
If there was any consolation at all, at least you could say Gary's death was quick.
Those who came next would not be so lucky….

***

Once The Grishnakka had finally ate its fill, and finished assimilating the bones of its latest victim, the monster paused where it stood and cocked its head, back the way it had come. With its preternatural hearing, the faint sound of voices and laughter could be heard, carried on the wind, from somewhere way over to the West, several miles away.
As it stood there, The Grishnakka thought it could also make out the faint light of campfires, presumably emanating from some kind of camp, somewhere off in the distance. Still hungry, The Grishnakka dropped to all fours, and started heading off in the direction of the Boy Scout Camp Jeremy, Robin and Gary had all been excluded from.
The deaths of the three boys had just been the beginning…
Before this night was over, many more would fall victim to *The Grishnakka…*

***

Chief Constable Grant Chambers was lying in bed, asleep, when his mobile phone started ringing beside him, waking him up from his slumber; it's flashing screen lighting up the bedroom with its bright, luminescent light as it rang.

Thankfully, the sound of his mobile phone's ringtone – the theme tune to ITV's The Bill - failed to wake up his wife. Instantly recognising the number calling him, Grant Chambers – still half asleep – picked up his mobile, and moved out of the bedroom and into the hallway to answer it.

As the resident Chief Constable of a small rural police force – largely made up of PCSO's and local volunteers – he was always on call, 24-7, but as the UK equivalent of a small town Sheriff, there was rarely any need for his sleep to be disturbed because out here, in this sleepy little Norfolk village, there rarely as ever any kind of trouble that required his attention.

Not tonight though. Tonight was different.

Because Chambers knew, the person currently calling him would only have done so at this time at night if there was a problem that only he would be able to deal with.

"Hello?" Chief Constable Chambers said, hitting the answer button immediately on his phone as he did so. "This is the Chief – what the hell's going on?"

"We have a problem," the person on the other end of the line told him, also speaking quietly as if not wanting to disturb whoever else might possibly be in the room with them. "I think you'd better get over here. Right away."

"What is it?" The Chief Constable asked, irritated. "Whatever it is, it had better be serious – waking me up at this time of night."

"It's the girl," the person on the other end of the line proceeded to tell him. "I don't know how it happened, honest I don't, but somehow she managed to get away. Somehow, she's managed to escape…"

"Fuck," Chief Constable Chambers cursed, already moving back into the bedroom and pulling on his uniform in the dark, taking it from where it sat on a chair in the far corner of the room. "Stay there, and I'll be right on my way…"

"Grant? What is it? What time is it? Was that someone on the phone? Who's calling you at this time?" His wife asked, from her side of the bed, still herself on the verge of being asleep.

"Nothing for you to worry about," Grant lied. He finished pulling on his shirt and trousers, and started to hurriedly do up the buttons. "You go back to sleep, I just need to pop out, that's all. I'll be back before you know it."

But his wife was already snoring, having instantly fallen straight back into sleep. Grant took one last, long look at her, then quickly exited the bedroom shutting the door very quietly behind him.

He had no idea his problems were only just beginning…or what kind of terror had already been unleashed on his town.

But he would soon.

Very soon.

Very soon indeed…

About the author

Mark Woods is a successful Chef of over thirty years who lives in Norfolk, England, where much of his work is set. He is the U.K horror author responsible for such novels as Time of Tides; Fear of the Dark; Arachnattack; Killer Cruise; Fear of the Dead; and The Golem. He was also one of six authors who contributed towards the creation of the vampire novel, Feral Hearts for J.E.A.

Also available from Black Hart Press by the same author

Fear of the Dead by Mark Woods

The Z-pocalypse starts here…and the end of days is finally upon us.
UK horror author, Mark Woods, here presents four tales of the Zombie apocalypse.
In 'Santa Clauz is coming to town', a man with a phobia of all things Christmas finds himself fighting off a horde of department store Father Christmas's when a zombie outbreak occurs.
In 'Solitary Confinement', a young woman does her best to protect her son, deep in the heart of Thetford Forest.
'Dairy of the Dead' tells the story of what happens when animals start to become infected on a remote dairy farm.
And in 'They came with the cold', three friends, out on a fishing trip, decide to head further North, hoping the cold will prevent the zombies from following, only to find themselves trapped with nowhere to go.

What people are saying about Fear of the Dead:
"Whilst you would think there wasn't room for yet another zombie story, Woods inserts just enough – normally via a certain dark humour – to make you carry on reading. All in all, an enjoyable zombie romp." Book reviewer, Steph Ellis.

Contagion – a Fear of the Dead novella by Mark Woods

The pandemic was just the beginning...
In the midst of a global pandemic, much of the world goes into lockdown...but the world's governments aren't telling the full story.
What they're not telling people is that the dead are coming back to life.
Following a series of Terrorist attacks all across the globe, the situation only gets worse and soon, the Dead begin to outnumber the living.
And for a small group of survivors, the nightmare is only just beginning...

What people are saying about Contagion.
"I gave this 5 stars because it was brill and kept me hooked. Minus the zombies, it was hard to keep remembering that we are currently living (through) this virus! Well done…would recommend!" Amazon reviewer, Samantha Devaney.

Fear of the Dark by Mark Woods

Sometimes it's not the dark you should be afraid of…it's what's hiding in it. Whilst helping an old man sort through all the junk up in his attic, a young boy discovers a photo of his elderly neighbour taken many years before. Sitting him down, the old man starts to tell him the tale of the night the photo was taken – a night, one Halloween, when he and five of his friends all sat down to tell each other scary stories…with terrifying and tragic results.

Time of Tides by Mark Woods

What if Global warning wasn't just down to climate change?
What if it was down to something else?
As the worst storm of all-time hits the entire globe, one family flees to the Norfolk Broads in order to escape, only to quickly discover that nowhere is truly safe. Now featuring two extra bonus short stories, Night Swimming and The Last Staff Party.

The Golem by Mark Woods.

Everyone thinks they know the story of the Golem – the ancient Jewish legend about a creature fashioned from clay and brought to life - but as one man is about to discover, the story people think they know is only just the tip of the iceberg.

Arachnattack by Mark Woods

What *is* The Project?
They called it The Summer of Spiders, and though there were those in later years who would go on to question just how much of what was actually reported, for those who lived through it that summer was one that no-one would ever forget...
In the small, sleepy Norfolk market town of Dyreham, something evil has been unleashed. When a crazed scientist unwittingly allows his army of genetically modified False Widow spiders to escape, it isn't long before the whole town quickly comes under attack.
Meanwhile, as a local reporter begins an investigation into the scientific research institute known as Greenacres, he soon discovers the spiders are just one small part of a much bigger conspiracy...

Killer Cruise by Mark Woods

Long before Arachnattack, there was the very first Project.

1942, the Second World War.

Behind enemy lines, Lance-Corporal Wilfred Bromley encounters an elite Nazi division that call themselves The War-Wolves and discovers the existence of Hitler's sinister secret project to create a preternatural army.

Many years later, long after the war, Wilfred is upon the cruise ship, The Bellastaria, when he soon finds himself once again fighting off both Vampyre and Werewolves when the ship he is on comes under attack. Fleeing to safety, and rescued by another passing ship, Wilfred is shocked to discover the project he long thought was dead is still very much up and running, and that the creation of The War-Wolves was just the very beginning…

Printed in Great Britain
by Amazon